WHEN THE LIVING
HAVE LOST

RICK WOOD

BLOOD SPLATTER PRESS

ABOUT THE AUTHOR

Rick Wood is a British writer born in Cheltenham.

His love for writing came at an early age, as did his battle with mental health. After defeating his demons, he grew up and became a stand-up comedian, then a drama and English teacher, before giving it all up to become a full-time author.

He now lives in Loughborough, where he divides his time between watching horror, reading horror, and writing horror.

ALSO BY RICK WOOD

The Sensitives
The Sensitives
My Exorcism Killed Me
Close to Death
Demon's Daughter
Questions for the Devil
Repent
The Resurgence
Until the End

The Rogue Exorcist
The Haunting of Evie Meyers
The Torment of Billy Tate
The Corruption of Carly Michaels

Standalones
When Liberty Dies
The Death Club

Chronicles of the Infected
Zombie Attack
Zombie Defence
Zombie World

Non-Fiction
How to Write an Awesome Novel
Horror, Demons and Philosophy

THE MONSTERS: MASKETES

Masketes are large flying monsters with long snouts, veiny wings, sharp fangs and curved, deadly claws. Large enough that you will see them from a distance, but fast enough that it won't make a difference—they are the true monsters of the sky.

Their diving precision makes them a threatening predator. Once they see their prey on the ground, they dive upon them with such accuracy of aim and expert speed that the fleeing prey can do little about it.

When they catch their prey, their claws dig deep enough into their food's body so their food doesn't squirm.

Not that they need to pick up their prey if they don't want to—their jaws are sharp enough that they could slice your head clean off on impact.

THE MONSTERS: THORALS

These four-legged, sturdy creatures are good hunters and quick to pounce—but their most terrifying feature is their appearance. Overwhelming in size, with red eyes and jaws that salivate the blood of their victims.

Their only weakness is that you can hear them coming from miles away—such is the earth-shaking thud that announces their presence.

Their sense of smell and hearing means they can detect prey from far off. Their teeth are curved and sharp and can slice through the thickest and toughest of meat.

THE MONSTERS: LISKERS

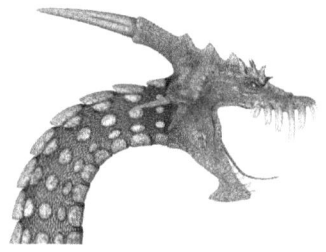

The scariest, most vile of all the creatures that crawled out the earth. They have long, snake-like bodies, thicker than an aged tree trunk and almost 5 acres long. These bodies are not only huge, but are coarse and rough; likely to draw blood should you scrape your skin against them.

These creatures are rare—but for those few that encounter them, they are deadly. Their fangs drip poison that paralyses their victim, meaning their food remains immobile as they devour it.

THE MONSTERS: WASTERS

They are not strictly monsters like Masketes, Thorals and Liskers, having been human once—but you should not underestimate these lethal hunters.

These are survivors of the apocalypse who took the coward's way out—choosing to become slaves to the creatures in return for their survival. As part of the deal, they also lost their consciousness, becoming mindless hunters and obedient servants.

Wasters rely on their cannibalistic appetites to survive—and once they spot the person they wish to consume, they will hunt as a pack to intimidate and catch their victim.

Not only to they have a desire to eat human flesh, they have a feral sexual appetite – meaning their victims will often suffer a horrific fate before it eats them alive.

CHAPTER ONE

CIA'S TRAINER, that was once white and was now a mixture of red and grey, lifts itself over a set of still stuttering lips; stuttering, of course, not because of breath that comes from life—but because of the gases released from the body after death.

She looks down at what she's done.

The silent remains of mayhem.

Lives formed from fake liberty and ended in glorious decay.

Blood that had been splashed like scattered dust, released from bodies the world had already forgotten.

Her knees hit the floor and her head hits her hands.

Again?

All of this... again?

What happened to hope? Optimism? To grabbing a larger glass and filling it until it was half full?

She hates herself.

Except, she doesn't.

She only *wants* to hate herself.

It was necessary.

But was it?

What is necessary anymore?

It is a different world. A different time. A time to celebrate the violent side of human nature, a time to dance upon the remnants of humanity.

Humanity had been a lie.

The end of the world had made that certain.

She has to push herself up. Take herself from her knees.

She has to find a way to her feet, regain her balance, and revive her muscles.

After all, it was her muscles that did this. How can they be so destructive one moment, then so lackadaisical the next?

"Nnnnnraaargh!"

She goes to scream *no* but doesn't allow herself the luxury. Her wail turns into a moan, then she hates herself for moaning, so she morphs it into a defiant scream.

Defiant of what?

Her own actions?

Who has killed more—the monsters or her?

Don't do that.

Don't compare her to a monster.

To be a monster would be to remove responsibility.

To declare yourself a mindless killer, to claim a personality disorder or even psychopathy; those were the excuses society had used, once upon a time, to excuse people like her.

She says she did this to protect herself.

To protect Boy.

To keep them both from harm.

And she had brought yet more harm to others as a result.

It was, what, 2,000 in the Sanctity?

And she did away with Dalton soon after.

And now this...

She would like to say they didn't deserve it, but no one deserves anything anymore.

Words like *deserve* and *right* and *wrong* are manmade.

And when man has fallen, those manmade declaratives are nothing but an aged ideology.

Once upon a time, mankind used god to explain the weather.

Once upon a time, mankind used demons to explain their actions,

And, once upon a time, mankind used words like *right* and *wrong* to try to bring some sense to senseless actions.

This isn't one way or the other.

It just is.

And once she has wiped the blood from her face, she will walk on once more into this world and never look back.

After all, she doesn't miss the father who had started this rage.

Maybe, someday, people will come to fear her as the fifth monster.

Then again, if someone saw the wreckage she was leaving, *monster* may not be strong enough.

THEN

CHAPTER TWO

RYKER PAUSED, taking a moment to regain his breath. Not that he needed to, the hill climb had done nothing to dent his stamina—but the girl was lagging far behind.

She was just a child, he reminded himself.

She was probably distressed from her ordeals, he reminded himself.

She would be useful to them, he insisted to himself.

"You all right?" he asked, though he didn't really care.

She said nothing.

She had said nothing the entire time they had been travelling.

"It's not far now," Ryker said.

She paused, the wind pushing her off her stride. It wasn't that windy, but she was tired and young and weak and for god's sake why was he even bothering with her?

Because Arnold insisted.

They needed to the young.

Ideally female.

Ideally in peak condition.

She wasn't old enough to bare child yet. They needed more children now, but with her they would have to wait.

Not long, he guessed. Her periods were bound to start soon.

But still too long for what the community needed.

Then again, Arnold wanted her for something else.

A child like her would be perfect for *the event,* and he couldn't imagine Arnold being patient enough to wait for her reproductive organs to develop before using her such a task.

He looked over his shoulder. She was still struggling up the hill. Having been lost in thought, he hadn't noticed just how long she was taking.

He waited and peered over the view. Looked over the world. Green fields next to wrecked farmhouses. Burnt-out buildings, but flourishing wildlife. It seemed that it was only what mankind had created that was destroyed. Nature was still the victor.

In the distance he heard a growl. Undoubtedly a Thoral.

He tried to see it. Strained.

And there it was, in the distance. Its giant body that didn't look so giant from up on this hill shook the trees, their leaves quivering under the strain of its pounding footsteps.

Ryker looked beyond the Thoral, into the distance, to where a young woman was, along with the bizarre boy she insisted on dragging behind her.

He wondered if the Thoral would get to them before he did. It was unlikely - they were still quite a distance away from the creature, and with the sound it was making, they'd no doubt pick up on it and divert their course.

He'd been following this woman for a while.

He'd seen what she'd done.

How she'd pinned a guy to the floor by his feet and hands.

Took him to the point of death, then hid inside as she let the Masketes finish him.

It was brutal.

It was deplorable.

It was *brilliant*.

They were running out of warriors. They needed someone with this savage mentality and taste for war. They needed a woman like this.

Shame about the boy, though.

Arnold would not want the boy.

Ryker was sure he could dispose of the strange child before they arrived back at the community. There were plenty of places to lose him, and plenty of hungry monsters to devour his pointless little body. They'd console her, then give her the role she could so aptly fulfil.

The girl finally reached his side.

No matter how useless that boy seemed, he'd find it tough to be as pathetic as this girl.

Ryker tried not to look at her with disgust. He was physically fit; he knew that—but she was a joke. He was so used to being on his own, scavenging, only occasionally recruiting.

But when the event comes around and Arnold makes his choices, community members tend to deplete in numbers quickly.

All for a good cause, of course.

Ryker took a bottle of water from his bag—the heavy bag he was carrying, compared to the *nothing* the girl was struggling up the hill with. He unscrewed the top and handed it to her.

She paused for a moment. Looked at it. Took it and gently sipped.

"Stop being so fucking dainty," Ryker commanded. "It's water, not whiskey. Drink it."

She did as she was told, then handed the water bottle back.

"So you going to talk to me or what?" he said, then looked to the girl expectantly.

"What's your name?" he tried.

She looked down.

"I've helped you, so talk to me. What's your name?"

She looked at him, her eyes so weary, so scared.

"I said what's your fucking name?"

"C—C—Cathryn."

"See, how hard was that Cathryn? What's your deal, then? Doubt you'd made it this long on your own. Not someone as out of shape and annoying as you are."

She looked back at him with her wounded expression. Maybe he was being a little harsh.

"Right, fine, sorry, I'm not used to talking to people. Well, I am—just not irritating kids who don't bloody talk. Where's your mum?"

She looked down.

"Your dad?"

She wiped her eyes.

"Ah, right. Dead. Yeah? That right? They dead?"

She nodded without looking at him.

"Fuck."

He took in a deep breath. Looked over the horizon once more. Knew that he should pretend to care, but let's be honest —everyone had lost someone. No one left alive had been left alive without suffering death and loss. In this world, they needed to get over it, and get over it fast, before they became a burden.

Footsteps approached, and Ryker finally saw the man he was waiting for.

"Hello, Hades," he said. "Which is a stupid name, by the way."

"I know," Hades replied, with a far more charming smile than Ryker's grimace. "You tell me that every time I see you."

"I mean, what, you the god of water or something? Seriously?"

"Hades was the god of underworld."

"I don't give a shit. This is Cathryn."

Hades smiled at Cathryn. Cathryn blushed.

Damn, how this guy always seemed to charm everyone. Ryker could barely get a word out of the girl, now she was blushing at this charlatan.

"You not coming?" Hades asked.

"Why, you scared to be on your own?"

"It's half a mile, I'll be fine. Besides, Cathryn will protect me."

He smiled at Cathryn. She blushed again.

This fucking guy.

"There's someone I need to go back for."

"Arnold didn't want more kids."

"This isn't a kid. It's a warrior."

"A man?"

"Young woman."

"Well, you do that. Come on, Cathryn."

Hades held his hand out. Cathryn took it and strolled away from Ryker, staying close to Hades.

Ryker sometimes wished he had Hades' charm. Then he realised it would mean becoming a weak little prick like him, and decided he was far happier being who he was.

He needed to control his temper, though. Cathryn had

wound him up, but he had a feeling he would need to be far nicer to coerce this woman to come.

He put on his smile.

Put on his nice voice.

Removed the curse words.

And began his descent down the hill.

CHAPTER THREE

THEY WERE HAVING a rest for Boy to eat some fruit, or so Cia had told him.

He sat peacefully, a few paces away, mindlessly scoffing a collection of grapes and apples that she had recently acquired.

This allowed Cia to have her breakdown without him watching.

She didn't know what it was, nor did she understand it, or want it—but it kept happening. Sometimes every few days, and sometimes every few hours. And now, it was as bad as it ever had been.

It had only started a few weeks ago.

Back when she had...

Dalton appeared before her and, even though she knew he wasn't there, she reached for him, swiping her hand through the man she had fallen in love with and forced to murder for the safety of her and Boy.

She was being smothered.

She wasn't—she was just sitting there, on a log, staring at an absent body, staring back at her. Yet it felt like a pillow was being held over her face, pushing down on her, squashing her breath. She panicked, despite there being nothing to panic for. She'd checked their surroundings. The tremble of a Thoral had passed, but it had been distant, and the ground had only shaken rather than seized.

But now she shook. Now she seized. She lifted her arms to head height, staring as they helplessly trembled, quivering and shivering and shaking and rocking and *why are they doing that...*

She tried stiffening them, but her shortness of breath caught her once more.

Boy had nearly finished his lunch, and she needed to regain control.

Was this because of what happened with Dalton? What she'd had to do to him?

Or was this because of what happened before? When she let monsters free to slaughter the sick and twisted minds of the sanctity—including her neglectful father?

Or was this because she was a bad person? Had these things turned her evil and this was her comeuppance?

But she had to remind herself: *evil doesn't exist anymore.*

There were no rules in place to dictate who one should and shouldn't kill, what one shouldn't steal, or what one should find ethical or corrupt. Laws had disappeared with most of the human race, leaving just as quickly as the minds who thought it up.

And now it was her. Sat on a log. Her heart bursting against the constraints of her chest.

A trickle of sweat trickled down her forehead and dropped into her eye.

She was freezing.

Cold, yet fiercely hot.

Empty, yet heavy and slow.

She went to stand and fell, collapsed to her knees, her hands landing in thick mud.

Funny, she used to care about things like mud. She used to hate getting mud on her hands or her clothes. She'd get a spec of dirt on her and have to go wash it off.

Now filth was a part of life. Wearing dirty clothes and washing sporadically. Living in the outdoors where flies would swarm around her face and she wouldn't even notice them.

Boy finished. Turned toward her.

She willed her breathing to return. She wheezed like the broken squeaker of a toy, coughed like there was something to cough up.

"Rosy?" Boy asked.

Sweet Boy. So wonderful, yet so unable to understand. If society was still intact, they would diagnose him with autism. They would claim he had a problem.

To her, he did not have a problem. If anything, his mind was more advanced than everyone else's. The things he could remember, recite and recall were beyond amazing; to her, it was everyone else's minds that were yet to evolve to the brilliance of his.

She raised an arm, presented a hand, and the arm fell just as quick.

"I'm fine," she lied.

He wouldn't know whether she meant it. He had no perception of subtext. If she said she was fine, she was fine— and his confusion came from how she did not seem fine. And she could see in his face how that confusion created such anxiety, that lack of ability to recognise what was going on when words and actions contradicted so much.

She closed her eyes. Forgot about the world for a

moment. Pushed Dalton from before her, allowed herself to breathe; *forced* herself to breathe.

In time, her heart slowed down, her sweating lessened, and her body's shaking turned from a furious shudder to a mild wobble.

She opened her eyes and Boy was next to her. His hand on her back.

"It's okay," she told him. She had to keep him calm, even if she couldn't keep herself calm.

She pushed herself to her feet. Gave him a smile and pretended to mean it.

"Did you have your lunch?" she asked.

Boy nodded.

"Was it nice?"

Boy nodded again.

"Which was your favourite fruit?"

"Grapes."

What she'd do for some grapes. She hadn't eaten properly in so long. They hadn't enough food to keep both of them fit and healthy.

They'd survived years together, but she wasn't sure how many more weeks they'd manage. All supermarkets had been ransacked and emptied of most of their contents, and what hadn't been looted was now covered in mould. They could pick some fruit, but even plants and trees with ripe food were dying with no one to take care of them.

She did not know how they would survive much longer.

She took his hand. He knew none of this. He didn't need to.

They had always found a way.

They just had to keep moving. What they were moving toward, and what she was moving from, she didn't know. It just felt like they needed to keep walking. Try to find somewhere that food would be easier to come by.

Even though that place would not exist.

"Let's go find somewhere to sleep for the night," she said, and led him forward.

She did not want Boy to have to suffer, but she was wondering how she could prevent that much longer.

She willed her mind to be quiet, as impossible as that was, and walked on.

That's when Cia heard it. The crunching of leaves, the unmistakable sound of breathing.

She kept walking, but also kept listening.

Getting ready.

They were not alone.

CHAPTER FOUR

THEIR TRACKS WEREN'T tough to follow. Wide strides of a smaller foot followed smaller steps of a longer shoe. Like she was marching forward, and he was always shuffling behind.

Such a liability.

Why did she bother?

Why risk her survival for him?

Ryker paused behind a tree and watched. The boy shovelled down fruit like it was the only thing left in the world.

And she was... well, Ryker wasn't sure.

She was sat on a log, staring wide eyed at the ground, rocking, shaking, unnoticed by the boy smearing grape juice all over his face.

He watched her intently, peering at her like she was a specimen beneath a microscope, and he was trying to learn what she was. Like she was a newly found amoeba, and he was studying her actions, deciphering what her actions meant.

For someone so brutal, so lethal with her actions, she so... weak.

She seemed to calm down as the boy approached her. She stood and said something to him, and they moved on.

It would be dark soon.

He would need to act now.

He moved from his hiding place and quickened his pace in their direction. He tried to keep quiet, but the leaves crunched beneath the lightest step, and he could see the girl pausing, her ears pricking, a glance over her shoulder.

She knew he was there.

So how was he going to do this?

He wished he'd thought about this more. Not that he feared her, but she had shown that she was willing to kill, and his defences would need to be ready.

He stopped trying to hide his steps. He walked briskly, away from cover, so they knew he was approaching.

The girl stopped.

She grabbed the boy's arm, curling his jumper up in his hand. The way she was holding onto him, it was as if he could fly away at any moment, and she was having to keep him on earth.

"It's okay!" Ryker shouted out.

The girl turned instantly. Her knife was out before Ryker could tell where it had come from.

"Please, put your knife away," Ryker continued. "I'm not here to hurt you."

He put his hands in the air and emerged into her eyeline.

She didn't shift, didn't move, didn't flinch. Just stared at him, her fingers gripping the handle. Her eyes didn't widen, and her body didn't lurch forward, nor did she back off or recede.

She was ready and able, mentally preparing herself for whatever fight was to come.

"Please, put the knife away," Ryker insisted.

She didn't.

She remained motionless, staring. The boy shifted position behind her, so she was between them, and peered over her head.

"Look," Ryker said, opening his jacket and showing his two knives. "I'm unarmed."

He removed the knives from the inside of his jacket and slowly crouched, placing them on the ground. He took another from his ankle and placed it beside them. He took a few steps away from the knives and toward the girl, keeping his hands in the air, moving slowly.

"I've removed my knives. I will not hurt you."

The closer he got, the more fire he could see in her. Her lip curled; her nose wrinkled into a snarl. She looked possessed by an animal, like a raging bull or untamed lion, ready to pounce, just waiting for the moment.

"My name is Ryker," he said.

Maybe if he was on first-name terms, that would humanise him, and she would stop. She would back down, allow him to explain.

"What is yours?"

She didn't answer. He edged forward again until he was just a few paces away. She did have the potential to be quite pretty; mixed race, black bushy hair, petite. She could probably still pass as a child. Yet her white vest was covered in mud, her arms were just as grubby, and bruises and wounds decorated her skin; if she were a house, the wallpaper would have peeled, and the walls would be crumbling.

"Please," Ryker said. "I'm not going to hurt you."

Another pause, and her knife dropped to her side. Tension left her body, she relaxed, and she even smiled.

"Fine," she said. "You can come closer."

He stepped forward. As soon as he was within her grasp

she took his legs out with the swipe of hers, landed a knee on his chest that winded him and, as he collapsed on a log, pressed the point of the knife against his throat. Just a push of half an inch and he would be gushing blood and suffocating.

He cursed himself for allowing himself to be fooled. She was a dainty little woman, and she had brought him down so easily.

He reminded himself not to fight back.

If he hurt her, that would only turn her against him more.

No, he would have to rely on patience; what little of that he had.

Though he wished he could just knock her out and tie her up.

But such a thing did not inspire trust.

So he allowed her to think she was in control.

Just until his patience truly ran out, then he would slaughter this bitch.

He took the small blade from the inside of his belt and readied it by her waist.

CHAPTER FIVE

EVERYTHING about the man was off.

His hair, his clothes, his skin...

It was all so...

Wrong.

His hair was a dark blond that didn't match his eyebrows. His skin was the kind of clean that only luxurious creams could provide. His clothes bore no rips, no tears, no mud or grease or holes. His swagger was that of a privileged white man, like those she met in the sanctity; he looked nothing like a ravaged soul struggling to survive against the elements and the monsters.

"Tell me..." she growled, her voice low and husky, far more intimidating than her petite stature should allow. "Who... you are..."

"I told you," the man said urgently, his voice full of a panic that gave Cia a glow of satisfaction. "My name is Ryker."

"Where do you come from, Ryker?"

"Let me go and I'll tell you."

She pressed the point of her knife a little more firmly against his throat.

"Tell me now," she commanded.

He stared back at her and, in his face, she saw his reaction to how she must appear. She was once a vulnerable child chasing her daddy through the country, and now she was something else. A woman who'd killed the only man she ever thought could help protect her and Boy, that could love her.

Caution was key to her survival, as was the fiery side of her she no longer kept contained; so she let him see her as a rabid beast, as a feral creature ready to strike—if that's how she needed to protect her and Boy, then that was how she would do it.

Slowly, his eyes floated away from hers, and looked over her shoulder, where she knew Boy was standing. She gripped the knife tighter and leant over him further.

"Don't look at him," she said. "Look at me."

"I can help you," he insisted.

"No one can help anyone."

"I can, I promise."

"Give me a reason why I shouldn't kill you."

His expression seemed to turn. The fear he presented abruptly turned to impatience and, before she knew it, he took her legs out from beneath her; she was on her back, one of his hands pinning down her knife hand while his other held a small blade by her throat.

Shit.

How could she be so stupid?

She looked at Boy, upside down, poised between trying to protect her and running to a tree to cover his ears and scream.

"It's okay," she told him. "Go sit on the log."

He feebly nodded, a worry he couldn't possibly understand taking hold of his body, and he did as she told him.

She turned to the man mounting her, holding a blade he had supposedly discarded to her neck.

"I thought you threw all your knives away."

He hovered the blade over her then stood, threw the blade away, and held his hand out.

"Now I have," he said.

She looked at his hand, glaring up at him.

"Come on," he said.

Reluctantly, she took his hand, and he helped her up. As soon as she was on her feet, she snatched her hand back.

And stood there.

Looking at him.

Awaiting his next move.

Wondering how she could kill him.

"Please," he said, supposedly patient and understanding, yet she could see that anger in his eyes. "Just listen to me."

She huffed, the only sign that she was listening.

"We have a community, a place where civilisation has remained, where we are protected. We want to invite you to a home there, to live."

Cia recalled the last community she was invited into. It had seemed pleasant enough, until she had learnt that they planned to impregnate her, along with all the other women, in an attempt to repopulate the earth. In the end, she'd had to allow herself to be fucked for her own survival—then she had killed the man in his grandest moment of pleasure and biggest moment of weakness.

"We're okay, thank you," she said, no hint of gratefulness to her statement.

"I really must insist," he persisted. "We really are kind people."

"There are no kind people."

"It would be a place for you, for him, to stay."

Cia looked over her shoulder at Boy.

She knew they didn't have much left. Resources were running out rapidly. She was so hungry, and so tired. Death was looking like a welcome way out at this point; their only prevention of future misery.

But how could she trust this man?

There were no good people anymore. Once the laws of the land came shattering down, as did the morals of the many.

"Just come and have a look," Ryker said. "Just come, look, and if you don't like it, if it seems not right to you, you can leave."

"How do I know you'll let me leave?"

"Look, this is a two-way thing—we want you to come, but to fulfil a purpose. Everyone has a role there. Yours is to be a warrior. To help protect us."

"I am no warrior."

"Oh, I beg to differ. I have seen how you survive."

"You've been following us?"

"I've been scouting you. Watching, to make sure you were what we needed."

She looked back at Boy who sat there, waiting, not understanding.

"And what about him?" Cia asked. "He isn't a warrior."

Ryker looked to be chewing over a conundrum. To be considering something deeply.

Little did he know his answer would determine whether she was to go with him.

"Then..." Ryker said. "Then, well... he can come. We can find a place for him too."

"As a warrior?"

"I am sure we can find another role for him to perform."

She concluded that they had little choice. She would go, but she would be wary.

"How far is it?"

"A few miles. Follow me."

She smiled at Boy.

"Come on," she said. He scuttled over and Ryker began leading them through the woods.

As soon as he took the first step, the ground shook.

Then another quake.

And another.

And another.

Cia and Ryker looked to each other.

"That's a Thoral," she said.

He walked over to where he'd thrown his knives and picked them up. She readied hers.

"Let's be quick," he said, and set off.

She followed.

CHAPTER SIX

WELL, that was an ordeal.

It was as if the girl didn't want a better life. Like she was happy roaming around the outside, fending for herself and this inept child. She was grubby and filthy, with dirt clinging to her arms and clothes like flies on shit.

He led them through the woods, hacking down branches and leaves as he did. He strode ahead, but he could hear her keeping pace behind him, just as he could see her shadow constantly checking behind her for the boy.

He knew that this boy was the reason for her hesitance. Just as he was the reason for her slowing them down, and for her aggressive response.

The boy had to go.

That was why he wasn't leading them to their civilisation. Not just yet.

That was why he was leading them toward the Thoral he had seen from the high point atop the hill.

Just a stop off to dispose of the wretched, needy freak; then onto their new home, with a new warrior, ready to replace those they'd lost. As irritating as she seemed to be, her cautious hostility would help kept the community safe.

Not against the monsters, of course. They did not need to fight them. It was the Wasters who caused them problems.

"Is it much further?" Cia asked.

"Not much," Ryker replied.

"Only Boy is struggling a bit."

Boy? His name was just... Boy?

He wanted rid of the kid even more.

"Maybe you could slow down," she suggested.

Maybe he could.

Maybe he didn't want to.

The ground trembled. A thundering quake spread through the soil, raising stones momentarily in the air, and sent each of them to their knees.

Now that wasn't the feel of a Thoral nearby.

That was the feel of a Thoral just around the corner.

He felt a little tinge of fear. The push of adrenaline when preparing for a fight.

But he was fine.

The Thoral wouldn't touch him.

"That's a Thoral," Cia said, turning to Boy to help him up.

Well done you fucking genius, he thought

"It is," he said, feigning surprise.

"Is there another way?" she asked.

"It would take us days to go around it," he said. "We have to go through."

"We're not risking it."

"It's worth the risk."

"I don't care. You and I can run, but Boy will freeze up when he sees it. We're not going past a Thoral."

Ryker bowed his head, clutched his sinus and sighed a huge sigh.

He went to speak, to feign sincerity and concern, but as soon as they stood up another shake of the earth forced them back to their knees.

Another footstep shook them, followed by another, and another, and they didn't bother getting up.

"It knows we're here," Cia said. "It's coming for us."

Ryker saw the terror in her face, not for herself, but for Boy. She held her hand out, pulled him close, and clutched onto him.

This kid would be harder to get rid of than Ryker had expected.

"Fine," Ryker said, knowing it was already too late. "We'll go another way."

They went to get up but stumbled to the ground again. The thuds became quicker, and the trees began to bustle with the oncoming snorts of a ruthless monster.

Cia didn't wait for Ryker. She grabbed Boy by the arm and dragged him, taking him back the way they had come. She remained crouched, forcing Boy to crawl, knowing the thuds would just throw her back to her knees.

Ryker looked behind him, willing the Thoral to appear, to get it over with.

He couldn't wait any longer. He followed Cia and Boy.

Just as Cia turned her head, just as she averted her gaze, Ryker grabbed a stick and threw it at Boy's legs. It stuck between his knees, tripping him, landing his head on a log.

Now Boy wouldn't move. He wouldn't get up. He was stuck, screaming, shaking his head, his eyes closed.

Cia tried to coerce him, but he wasn't listening.

Ryker ran ahead, then turned and looked back as the drooling, menacing, sickening head of a monumentally large, carnivorous beast appeared from the trees.

"Leave him," Ryker urged Cia. "It's too late. We have to go."

CHAPTER SEVEN

"NOT A CHANCE," Cia refuted.

She sat before Boy, putting a hand on each arm.

"Boy, listen" she whispered.

He was shouting, breaking down, refusing to believe what was happening. This was what he did; when something he couldn't handle happened, danger he couldn't understand, he shut himself away. He covered his ears, shouted, shook his head. So many times she had resigned herself to death, believing she would be killed trying to coerce him to move rather than saving herself.

This time would be no different.

"Boy," she whispered again, knowing he couldn't hear her, but knowing that the moment she lost her calm was the moment she stood no chance of getting him back.

"We need to go," Ryker insisted.

Cia ignored him.

The putrid, warm snort of the Thoral's breath upon her back made her shake. She readied herself for death, for the possibility of being snatched, taken, ripped apart by this creature.

Ryker leapt over her, toward the creature.

What the hell was he doing?

Risking himself for her?

But a glance over her shoulder showed no risk at all. It was if the Thoral stopped advancing. As if it saw him and ceased its attack.

Before she could watch any more, Boy shouted even harder, and she turned back to him.

Cia was sure she didn't see Ryker calm the beast. There was no way it just chose not to attack because he was there.

She was seeing things.

Ryker must be fighting it.

Either way, she couldn't look back. She had something far more important and far more precious to deal with.

She cupped Boy's face, stroked his cheeks, kissed him gently on the forehead and rested her head there.

"Come on, Boy, listen to me," she urged.

His eyes opened briefly, and she took the opportunity to look into them, to hold his face so he had to look back.

"It's okay," she said.

He cried and went to cover his eyes again, so she did the only thing she knew could work.

"The devil has departed," she began; reciting the poem only they shared. "And you are not alone."

Slowly, his cries stopped.

His eyes wandered toward the Thoral, and she quickly moved her head so he was looking at her.

"Take time to rebuild..."

"... our love in our home," Boy finished.

"That's good. So good. You're doing so well."

She kissed his forehead again, clasped his cheeks in her hands, looked into his eyes.

"Now get up."

Without giving him a choice, she stood, grabbing him by the hand.

She turned back to Ryker, who stood there, alone. The Thoral behind him somehow... gone.

"How did you do that?"

He took out a gun and presented it.

"Shot this."

"But I didn't hear any gunshots."

Ryker shifted, looking vaguely uncomfortable. Cia waited for an explanation, but Ryker put the gun away and walked on.

"We need to hurry," he said. "It'll be dark soon, and the Thoral will no doubt be back."

He walked.

She had questions, but they could wait. For now, she had to care for the most important thing in her life.

She led Boy by the hand, walking in Ryker's footsteps, expecting the Thoral to jump out at any moment.

It didn't.

CHAPTER EIGHT

LIKE A LION LOOKING over his kingdom, Arnold looked out of his office window to see his small town moving swiftly, everyone carrying out the chores they had been allocated. It worked in perfect synchronicity, everyone with their purpose, everyone scuttling about like ants serving their leader.

Although, Arnold was no lion. A lion is fierce, courageous, and commands respect from the animal kingdom.

Arnold was not the leader of this town based on power—he was the leader based upon financial superiority. Six months before the monsters had risen, a small portion of the human race already knew what was about to happen. The knowledge gave this elite few the opportunity to enter the Sanctity, an underground fortress designed to protect them whilst the weak perished.

Arnold had figured—why be one of the elite in the underground bunker, when he could be the only elite amongst the inferior?

So he'd bought a town. Acquired every building and offered surplus amounts of funding to the counsel. He had it fortressed by a large brick wall, protected and ready.

It was a town that was once known as Frome.

They all thought he was crazy, but when word of the monsters rising spread throughout Frome, the people had no choice but to recognise his leadership. If he had facilitated their survival then, as far as he was concerned, he owned them.

Years later and, last he heard, the Sanctity had fallen, and he was the leader of the only remaining civilisation in the country—possibly the world, for all he knew.

He knew he had made the right choice.

He returned to the reinforced leather seat behind his grand antique desk, taking a decanter from the dresser behind him and pouring a generous dose of gin into his crystal glass. He took it neat, as that was how his father had taught him— his father would have slayed a dragon before ruining good gin with ice. Ice was made from water, which was cheap and easy to come by, and this gin was not. Drinking it neat meant you gave it its due respect.

A rumble told him that the grand entrance to the town was being opened. He took his gin to the window, peered out, and saw Ryker, returning with others. A woman. And a boy.

The woman, who looked somewhere between black and white but not quite either, was filthy. Her walk did not match her stature; she strutted in like she was a lethal predator, whilst her size would suggest she was a dainty mouse. The boy beside her was even more bizarre, shuffling along with his head to the side, muttering. Something was wrong with him, probably a head case, who knew, who cared—if anyone did not serve a purpose in this town, he knew how to give them a purpose.

He straightened his tie, smoothed down his collar, and opened the window, looking down upon the street below.

"Ryker," he said as Ryker led the newcomers past. He

attempted to make his voice commanding, but it came out upper class and articulate in a way a rich person cannot fake. Money may not be a commodity one values anymore, but Arnold still spoke as if he still had the wealth he had had before.

"Arnold," Ryker acknowledged. "This is our town leader," Ryker told the other two.

The boy didn't look, but the puny, feral woman did. She glanced upwards, her scowl serious and her face not faltering.

"Once you have our new friends settled, please bring them to meet me," Ryker instructed. "I would love to meet them."

"Of course," Ryker said, and led them onward.

The girl glanced over her shoulder before she turned the far corner, passing the first set of vegetable patches and a small shop they used as a butcher.

Her glance was menacing, like she was sizing him up, a glare that could not be tamed.

He wasn't sure what to make of this one. He had instructed Ryker to find a warrior and, whilst she did not have the stature of a fighter, she clearly had the temperament. Only time would tell if she would prove useful.

As for the boy...

Why the hell did Ryker bring that useless bit of filth back here?

He did not look like a warrior and, if Ryker determined that he did, Arnold would have to seriously call into question Ryker's future judgement. There were few people he trusted in this town as much as Ryker, and he was sure there must be an explanation.

Arnold returned to his desk and refilled his glass.

He looked over his desk, as if there was paperwork to go over, like he was back in the old days of being a politician.

But this was a different kind of politics now.
Being a leader afforded one a different kind of power.

CHAPTER NINE

It was a surreal experience. To see so many people performing menial jobs and ardent tasks, just walking around like there wasn't a world gone to shit outside the walls.

It felt wrong.

Just like it had at the Sanctity.

So many people living their lives as if the horrors were far away, each person blissfully convinced that suffering did not exist.

Cia reminded herself not to prejudge the place. The Sanctity was different. It was a place that gave the rich elite their safety and denied her entry for the colour of her skin; despite her dad happily entering without her.

These people did not seem like politicians, wealthy racists, or like they had inherited a generous trust fund. Yes, this was another presumption, but they weren't walking around with the air of arrogance they had in the Sanctity; as if each step was treading over another piece of filth they owned. The people before her wore ill-fitting clothing as they sweated over crops or carried meat or fulfilled some other strenuous task.

"What is this place?" Cia asked.

"It's our home," Ryker answered.

"I mean... how?"

"How what?"

"How have you maintained something like this for so long, especially without being attacked by any of the creatures?"

He seemed to ignore the latter question.

"It used to be Frome," Ryker said. "A small town in southwest rural England. Now it's..." He held his arms aloft. "... Home."

Around another street corner a manmade patch of grass ran up the middle of the pavement, home to a dozen varieties of vegetable. Around another corner were fences around cattle and livestock. Some buildings even looked like shops: a sweet shop, a butcher's, a hairdresser...

It was an image Cia had forgotten. It felt like a far-off childhood dream.

"Let me show you to your home," Ryker said.

"A home?"

"Yes. With a shower."

A shower?

Pouring hot water instead of cold, dirty lakes?

She held onto Boy's hand and kept him close. She'd learnt the hard way that if something was too good to be true, then it normally was. For all she knew, Ryker could be leading them into a trick or an ambush, and she would need to have Boy next to her to protect him.

But it wasn't a trick or an ambush they stopped at.

It was a house. Brick, windows and a front door.

Cia marvelled at the sight. She hadn't seen a house still intact since her and her father left theirs. There were curtains in the window rather than moss, a welcome mat rather than rats, and she could even see wallpaper inside instead of the charred remains of a burnt-out living room.

Then something even stranger happened.

The door opened, to reveal a young girl stood looking at them.

Cia recognised the girl, but where from she couldn't tell. A vague familiarity struck her, but Cia couldn't know her, Cia didn't know anyone.

"Cathryn?" Boy said.

Cathryn...

Then she realised.

They had stopped briefly with a man named Colin, whom Dalton had murdered in his attempt to get to her and Boy. Colin's daughter had run away, left to fend for herself at barely a year younger than Boy. Cia had no idea where she went, and now...

"Oh my God," she muttered.

Ryker beamed next to her. "I think someone wants to say hello."

Cathryn ran toward Cia and leapt into her arms. Cia dropped to her knees and held Cathryn tight, fighting tears from her eyes. She had only known this girl a few hours, and she did not understand why it affected her so much, but it did.

Maybe because she had decided she was responsible for Cathryn's death, and it was a relief.

Maybe it was because Cathryn was another person who knew her, and if these people had kept her safe, then she could trust them.

Or, maybe, it was just pure joy at seeing this girl alive.

"I'm so sorry," Cia whispered into Cathryn's ear. "I'm so sorry about your..."

She couldn't say it.

Cathryn's young eyes looked into Cia's and she said softly, "It's okay, you're here now."

Cia hugged her tightly once again and whispered into her ear: "Are you safe? Have these people hurt you?"

Cathryn shook her head.

"They saved me," she said.

Cia hugged her more, then stood, wiping her eyes.

"Before you get settled," Ryker said, "I know that our town leader would love to meet you."

"Okay," Cia said, not in any fit state to argue.

"You can leave these two here to play if you wish, they will be safe–"

"No, they come with us," she said. "Both of them."

CHAPTER TEN

RYKER LED Cia back through the town with Boy and Cathryn trailing behind her, past the same sights that were just as astonishing as when she had entered minutes ago.

Even more astonishing was the building he led her to.

Over what used to be a road were a few rectangles of white leading to this building; a crossing, Cia remembered it being called. The building itself looked like it should crumble and fall, but its classical architecture still held firmly in place. They had even mounted a clock atop the right-hand side, displaying a time of day that didn't matter anymore; to Cia, it was the sun rising, in the middle of the sky, or setting—those were her times of day.

Ryker led her up the stone steps and through a room with a fireplace, large, grand windows, and a pristine tiled floor. Up another set of stairs, her feet tapped lightly on a marble floor that led to an impressive set of doors.

Ryker tapped on the door which was met with a gleeful, "Come in." He opened the door to reveal a man with white hair, a small tuft of beard, and a perfectly pressed, impressive suit.

"Thank you, Ryker," the man said, and Ryker backed out. He went to close the door, but Cia stopped him.

"Wait," she said, Boy and Cathryn still outside it.

"They will be right out here with me," Ryker said. "I promise."

The doors were closed before Cia could object any further. She tried to relax, knowing Boy was just on the other side of that door, and with Cathryn as company, but it bothered her immensely.

"Your little brother?" the man asked.

Cia looked back at him. His voice sounded like the perfect product of private education. His articulacy and his wealth were so clear in just a few words.

"No," Cia said, and added nothing further.

"Surely you're too young for him to be your son?"

"Correct," Cia said.

"So, please, tell me how it is you two have come by each other. Cousin? Friend of a close family? Child you used to babysit for, maybe?"

Cia didn't feel like giving him any information. She looked around the office instead, judging him by the many shelves of expensive ornaments. A crystal jug, a gold-plated globe, a certificate of an honorary degree from Oxford—but not a single picture frame.

"This is an impressive office," Cia said.

"You really think so?" Arnold answered, smiling, leaning toward her a little too enthusiastically. "I do hope it's not overdone."

"Of course not. Why wouldn't you have a room decorated with all this shit while the entire world is dying?"

"Ah," the man said, nodding. "You're one of them."

"One of what?"

"Let me just ask you, my dear—does it make sense to

reduce your own frivolities because somewhere in the world someone else is suffering? Before this happened, would you have stopped watching your television because someone, somewhere, could be starving?"

She glared at him, seething. Oh boy, she hated him.

"I do believe I am yet to introduce myself," he said. "My name is Arnold."

She nodded.

"And how should I address you?" he asked.

She hesitated. She realised she was still loitering by the door. She could hear Boy and Cathryn giggling faintly behind it, and that gave her reassurance.

"Cia," she said.

"Cia, what a lovely name. And do you have a last name?"

"Does it matter?"

"Why, I guess it does not. But it's always nice to know. Please, won't you come in, have a seat."

Arnold indicated the chair opposite his desk as he sat in his chair behind it. Cia paused, then trudged slowly to the chair, and sat on its edge.

"What do you think of the town?" Arnold asked. "Impressive, isn't it?"

"Sure."

"Do you not think so?"

Cia huffed. She didn't know what to think.

"I think it's odd how a community survived the initial attack, and the many years after it."

"Fortunately, the government granted a few of us the knowledge of the initial attack in time to do something about it. I found this town, bought it, and immediately had a wall built around it. Everyone thought I was mad. Now they are grateful."

"Must be lucky, getting to be one of the special ones who knew the world was about to end."

"My dear, look out the window at the many people working hard in this community—they would not have survived was it not for my knowing what was going to happen. The government could have told everyone and inspired panic or told a few and inspired grand actions of protection."

This guy had an answer for everything. Every time she had another qualm or contention, there he was with another well-prepared answer. He'd probably spent the last few years rehearsing them, preparing his excuses whilst those outside of his walls suffered.

"Forgive me," said Arnold, "but it seems as if you are angry that we have had this community here, thriving, whilst you have evidently been struggling out there?"

Precisely.

"I may be making an assumption, but if that is what you are thinking, I would ask you what else you would expect. Do we break down and plunge ourselves into a pit of misery because a stranger we don't know is having a hard time, or do we try to make the best out of a bad situation?"

"A bad situation?"

"You are here now, are you not?"

"Why?"

"I beg your pardon?"

"Why? Why am I here? I wouldn't be here unless you needed me here for something."

"Ah, yes. I presume Ryker mentioned what your role will be?"

"A warrior. Whatever that means."

Arnold clasped his hands together and leant his chin upon them.

"The biggest threat we have to this community are the Wasters. They hate us, and they often come to attack. We have ways of detecting when they are coming near; people on watch, for example—when they come, we need people to go out and dispose of them."

"You want me here to kill Wasters? Have you ever faced a Waster?"

"Not myself, personally, no. I understand they are tough to kill—but you would not be alone, and you would not be without weapons. I promise you the risk is minimal."

"What about the other monsters?"

A silence followed.

"I don't follow," Arnold said.

"The Thorals, the Liskers, the Masketes. What about them? What about when they attack?"

Arnold smiled a knowing smile that she was sure he intended to be reassuring, but only made her more concerned.

"You let me worry about them," Arnold said. "We have our ways of repelling them. It's the Wasters you need to focus on."

Cia went to question further, but before she could, a noise outside of the door attracted her attention. She left the office to find Boy grabbing a small cut on his knee.

"He fell," Cathryn said.

"It's fine," Cia said.

"Let me show you back to your home, there are plasters there," Ryker said.

Plasters?

After all they had endured, after the wounds they had suffered, it seemed a little pathetic to apply a plaster.

"He'll be fine," Cia said. "He's tough. And we know our way back, thank you."

Cia grabbed Boy's hand and led him away, Cathryn following. She glanced back at Arnold briefly as she turned the corner, watching him watching her. Something about his knowing look was unsettling.

But, then again, Cia knew she'd adapted to an environment where caution could save their life.

This was a situation where she could not tell whether to trust her instincts anymore.

CHAPTER ELEVEN

NIGHT DESCENDED, and it was time for Cia to go to her room.

Something she'd thought she'd never do again. She felt uneasy, not just by how it didn't seem real—the last time she'd had a room of her own, her father would say goodnight before she went to it. Her father, who betrayed her. Her father, who she had...

She banished all thoughts of death and violence and tried to replace them with promise. With positivity. With hope.

Hope wasn't an easy thing to find.

But maybe, at some point, she would find some here.

There were so many people doing things to help their community—something bad people wouldn't do. Maybe she should relax a little; let it be.

After all, Cathryn had seemed happy. Cia briefly met the young couple Cathryn was staying with a few streets away, and Cathryn couldn't have seemed more content.

Which was why she allowed Boy to sleep in his own room.

She had said goodnight, recited their poem a few times, and gone to leave. She paused by the door, looking in at him.

He was a teenager now.

She tried to recall herself entering her adolescence. She was a dork. A geek. An outcast.

It was a different person from a different time.

"I'm going to leave this door open," she said. "And I will be in the room next door. If anything happens, anything at all, come and let me know, and I'll..."

Boy's eyes were closed. His breathing was deep. He wasn't listening. He was sleeping. Such marvellous conditions allowed for a quick, deep slumber. He wasn't used to a mattress, or a pillow, or a duvet.

Such frivolities seemed bizarre. She could get used to them—but she had prepared herself for better conditions before, and it hadn't turned out well.

Was she right to be so pessimistic? Or was she just a prison of her experiences?

Without a society to contain the bad, the good become the bad.

But maybe this was society. A resemblance of it, at least. People performing specific tasks with specific functions, with a leader, and people cooperating with one another.

She loitered in the doorway, hesitant to let him out of her sight. She had regretted letting him out her sight before...

There I go again.

More assumptions that everything will go wrong.

She had pulled herself away from the door, leaving it open, and took the few steps into the next room along. She left the door open and walked into the room, pausing by the bed.

She looked at it.

The sheets were white. The duvet was blue. The pillow was big and soft.

She wanted to get into it, but to do so was to admit...

What?

What was she admitting?

What was she fighting?

Maybe she didn't want to allow herself to get used to these conditions. If she did, it would make her less lethal, less tough. She had survived on her tenacious spirit and cruel, cautious mind—would a life of comfort strip her of those? Then, when she would inevitably return to life outside those walls, she would...

She sighed.

Shook her head.

She pulled back the duvet. Sat on the bed.

The mattress sank in response to her pressure. She willed herself to lie down, to embrace the softness of the bed, its warmth, its security.

She did.

Awkwardly.

Laying on her side, pulling the duvet over her, forcing herself not to enjoy the pleasures it brought her.

But she sank into it, further into the bed, more comfortable than she ever thought possible.

Just as her eyes began to close, she opened them and leapt from the covers.

She listened, making sure Boy was okay, that she heard nothing.

Silence.

It was just what she was used to, that was all. There was nothing there.

She pulled back a curtain and peered out of the window

to see the darkened, empty streets, absent of blood and guts and danger.

She opened her bag.

Removed her knife.

Marvelled at its blade. Curved and sharp.

She lifted the pillow and placed the knife beneath it.

She allowed herself to return to bed and find her way back beneath the covers.

She sunk further and further into the comfort until, eventually, she found herself soundly asleep.

NOW

CHAPTER TWELVE

The corridors of a makeshift school...

She had walked past this place in the days after she'd arrived in the community.

She had seen children learning. It was a place where the young had thrived to learn once more.

Silly people, thinking they could recreate things as they once were.

When a house gets ripped apart by fire, you cannot rebuild it brick by brick. You could look for the foundations, you could try to recreate it; but you could not create the same rooms, the same memories, the same feelings...

This world is that house.

And for them to think they could recreate something as simple as a school...

It seems preposterous now.

But she had entertained it, even for a short time.

She thinks back to her childhood. To when she had considered school to be the worst thing forced upon her. Back when a strict teacher was the worst thing to fear.

She had hated it.

Not that she hadn't enjoyed learning new things—in fact, quite the opposite. She found herself in every top set, excelling especially at science, as she was bound to do with her father being such a profound scientist. She was destined to follow his path, to produce marvellous experiments in laboratories, produce a ground-breaking thesis for her PhD, to even make discoveries that would shake the way we perceive our world.

But school wasn't the building blocks for her—it was the rope around her chest. It was broken lockers, dirty looks and tiles of doom. The corridor was the walk to the gallows. It didn't set her free or give her the learning she needed, it just taught her what she already knew.

And wasn't she resented for it!

As any child entering their early teenage years would be, other students were envious of her talent. Their arduous trying failed while her instinctive abilities flourished. They begrudged her for it and boy did they let her know.

Staring at the charred remains of broken chairs and bloody tables, the classroom brought back one specific memory that Cia couldn't help but relive.

"A black hole," spoke Mrs Orchard, "is a bizarre thing."

Cia had loved black holes. They were fascinating.

Yet, as she looked around the classroom, she saw one boy stifling a yawn and a girl secretly painting her nails beneath the table.

"And which theory tells us about their mass, can anyone remember?"

The general relativity theory, Cia thought.

Mrs Orchard awaited an answer. Twenty-five dumb stares responded.

"Come on, we did this last week," Mrs Orchard insisted. "What is the theory, and what does it suggest?"

The general relativity theory, and that a compact mass can deform space-time into a black hole.

"Fine," Mrs Orchard said, giving up.

A girl across from Cia showed her friend a text message beneath the table, and they giggled together.

Cia could not for the life of her figure out why they did not find this interesting! This is space, black holes, the rules of the universe and beyond—and they were more interested in some dumb boy flirting via a wasted text message.

"It was the general relativity theory," Mrs Orchard finally said. "And it says that a compact mass can deform space-time into a black hole."

The two girls giggled again, then the one showing the text message smiled cheekily at a boy across the classroom, then they stifled another giggle like a bunch of mute hyenas.

"And what does a black hole do to the gravitational pull?"

Strengthens it.

"Come on, what does it do?"

Cia huffed.

This was fascinating, and her dad had taught her it, and she wanted to hear it again.

Yet everyone else would rather stare at a phone or their nails or, as with one guy, sniff their arm pits then fall asleep on their bag.

"Cia," Mrs Orchard announced, prompting Cia's entire body to stiffen.

She really, really hoped Mrs Orchard wasn't about to ask her the question.

Her eyes widened. Her heart thudded. She shook. She wanted to shrink away and have the ground swallow her up, or maybe even a black hole that would destroy everyone else in the classroom with it.

"Surely you know," Mrs Orchard prompted.

Yes, I do.

"What does a black hole do to gravity?"

Speeds it up so that nothing, not even light, can escape it.

The answer poised on the edge of her lips.

Then she looked around.

The girl had stopped painting her nails.

The girls had stopped looking at texts.

The boy had lifted his head from the sleeping position on his bag.

Everyone was looking at her. Smugly. Waiting for her to be the know-it-all they all presumed she was going to be.

She wanted to give the answer.

Hell, she'd settle for just saying something.

But she just stuttered.

And everyone grinned. Satisfied at her apparent lack of knowledge. Deliriously happy at her inability to form words, at her cripplingly introverted nature.

"Cia?" Mrs Orchard prompted again.

Cia went to speak, but didn't, and gave a shrug so small it probably went unnoticed.

"Fine," Mrs Orchard said. "A black hole speeds up gravity to such a speed that even light cannot escape it."

I knew that.

Cia bowed her head, let out a breath, and hated herself for being so smart, yet being so dumb.

And now, standing over the remnants of a school built by hands and destroyed by fire, she realises how little it mattered.

This classroom is decorated with the corpses of ambitious minds eager to learn.

Because that world is burnt to ashes, and not even the foundations survived.

No one cares if a child can read or write anymore.

No one cares about black holes or gravitational pulls.

No one cares about space exploration.

Thousands of years of scientific knowledge are gone, just like all the memories of homes and loving times the dead took with them.

A school where they teach you to read does not help in this world.

The only lesson they should have taught a student is how to survive—something none of these children have managed.

If only they had been taught the things that mattered.

Like being able to run, or fight, or kill.

And, looking around at the remnants of a classroom transformed an image of death within minutes, it is clear they had not known enough.

Cia has the education she needs.

She can run.

She can fight.

And, boy, could she kill.

THEN

CHAPTER THIRTEEN

CIA WAS ALMOST SURPRISED to wake up the next day. As soon as she was aware enough to know where she was and what had happened, she felt for the knife beneath her pillow.

It was still there.

She propelled herself out of bed and marched to the room next door, panicking. Anything could have happened to Boy.

But nothing had happened.

Boy slept soundly in his bed.

She remained in the doorway, watching him. She couldn't help but smile. He was peaceful, sleeping the best sleep he'd probably had in the time she had known him. He never slept in, but here he was, still unconscious.

"Hey," Cia said.

Boy's eyes slowly opened. He looked around with the same confusion she'd awoken with, then looked to Cia with a sleepy smile.

"Rosy?" he said.

"Yeah," Cia replied, her smile widening even further. "Remember where we are?"

He looked around the room then nodded.

She smiled an even bigger smile. She felt a feeling she hadn't felt before, an overwhelming surge of lightness—perhaps, to the person more accustomed to such feelings, they would call it happiness.

"Want to go check on Cathryn?" Cia asked. "See how she is?"

Boy nodded. He was so sleepy. It was adorable.

"I'll meet you downstairs."

She made her way down the steps that barely creaked or sunk beneath her step. The walls were so intact, the carpet so soft, the house so quiet; it was so strange. Even stranger, was the kitchen with cupboards full of food.

Most of it was stuff the community had grown. Bananas, apples, carrots and so forth. There was also some bread, and some tinned food.

She took a banana, unpeeled it and took her first bite.

Many years ago, if you'd have told Cia she would relish the taste of a fresh banana, she would have told you to go away and get her some chocolate. But now, it was delectable; so different to the rotting or expired food she was used to.

Boy came into the kitchen. She gave him a banana and watched him devour it with the same surprised pleasure she had.

And, after throwing their banana skins into the recycling bin—yes, they had a *recycling bin*—they entered the streets.

It was already busy with people carrying boxes of fresh produce, two men carrying a dead hog, one person even leading a class of children in perfect formation.

It was surreal. It was perfect. It was paradise.

"Come on," Cia urged Boy, taking him by the hand and leading them through the crowds of people.

After they'd turned the corner and past a few people

harvesting some crops, she arrived at the home where the young couple were taking care of Cathryn.

She knocked then turned and beamed at Boy, so pleased that Boy would get to play with another kid; something he'd never really experienced. It was too late for her, but maybe Boy could still regain some of his childhood.

When the door opened, however, the grim faces that met her told her it would not be happening. That something was wrong.

The couple stood with their arms around each other, as solemn as they could be.

"What's going on?" Cia demanded.

Ryker appeared behind them.

"Ryker, what is it?"

"Perhaps you two should talk alone," the man said. "We'll watch your boy."

Reluctantly, Cia allowed Boy to go with them into the living room and followed Ryker into the kitchen. She could still see Boy through a few panes of glass in the door, so she knew he was safe—meaning she could focus her attention solely on Ryker.

"What is going on?" she snapped.

Ryker hesitated. Sighed.

"Tell me!" Cia said. "Where is Cathryn?"

"During the night," Ryker said, slowly and cautiously. "She, er... she ran away."

"What?"

No.

Not possible.

Cathryn would not run away.

"She kept saying she wanted to find her dad," Ryker continued.

"Her dad is dead. She knew this."

Did she know this?

Did she see him die before she ran?

Cia's memory of the event was a little hazy. Could she be so sure?

"They put her to bed, telling her she would get to see you again in the morning," Ryker continued. "Then they woke up during the night to see her running."

"Well, where did she go?"

"Some people were coming back in through the doors, and she ran past them."

"Well, did anyone chase her?"

"Of course they did."

"And?"

Ryker shrugged. "I don't know what to tell you."

"The truth."

"She kept running, and they lost her."

"Why would she keep running if they were trying to help her?"

"You're not listening, Cia. She was adamant she was going. They kept trying to say they would help her, but she just kept running."

"How on earth would she outrun your guardsmen? Are they not trained?"

"Yes. It is unfortunate."

"Unfortunate!"

Cia threw her arms into the air and turned around.

"We sent another team out to find her this morning. They came back a few minutes ago. Nothing."

"When did this happen?"

"About midnight."

"Midnight! Why did no one tell me?"

"Cathryn was not your responsibility, she was this couple's–"

"Yes, she damn well was. Her dad is dead because of me, and she was my resp–"

Cia cut herself off. Turned around. Covered her face in her hands, then turned back decisively.

"I'm going out to look for her."

"Cia, we have sent trained men out to find her. If they haven't found her, then…"

"I don't care. I'm going out to find her."

"And what about your boy? Are you going to risk his life out there too?"

She paused.

He was right.

She wouldn't let Boy stay here alone, not yet.

At the same time, she didn't want to risk his life out there if she didn't have to.

Then again, they'd spent so long out there surviving, surely he could endure another few hours…

But at his speed she wouldn't get far. He'd slow her down too much, and the search would be futile.

The debate raged around her mind. She changed her mind one way to another, then back again, unable to settle on a single decision.

"Cia, I know this is tough."

Cia scoffed.

"Do you think we wanted her to go?" Ryker said.

Cia glared at his turning defensive.

How dare he?

He knew nothing of what they had suffered. He had no right to be defensive.

Cia looked through the door at Boy, playing happily with a box of Duplo. He organised the red bricks, the blue bricks and the green bricks into different piles, then arranged the piles into perfect symmetry.

He sure did have an extraordinary mind.

"I know this is tough," Ryker said.

"Do you?" Cia snapped.

"We've lost people before. It's heart-breaking. But it's always been down to their decisions. You are not responsible for this."

Wasn't she?

If she hadn't been responsible for Cathryn, who had been?

This couple?

Great job they did!

"Cia," Ryker said, forcing her to look at him.

She looked back at him expectantly, then he said those two words that concluded the issue and left Cia knowing that she had to think with her head, not her heart.

Those two words that let her know Cathryn was gone; that allowed her to know that there was no way she could track her and be sure of Boy's safety at the same time.

Those two damn words.

"She's gone."

CHAPTER FOURTEEN

It was agreed that Ryker would check in with Arnold.

Ryker was responsible for recruitment–but recruitment was a difficult task, and one that Arnold would not leave without supervision. Who knows what kind of miscreant or psychopath this world may have produced? How could Arnold sleep soundly, not fully knowing who was living in the community he had built, back when having a fortune meant something.

Do not be mistaken, he trusted Ryker

He just did not trust Cia.

"Well?" said Arnold as he heard Ryker's footsteps approach the open door, a door that was so rarely open; Arnold's desire for Ryker's report on the girl forced him to leave the door open, as if this would somehow encourage Ryker to hurry.

"The child's not a problem," Ryker announced.

"I was not asking about the child."

Ryker wiped sweat from his brow. It was a hot morning, and he had rushed up here, knowing he was already running late.

Arnold turned from the window and took in Ryker's dishevelled appearance.

"Don't tell me you're starting to like her," Arnold said.

"Like her? She's a good fighter. She might not look it, but she's spent the last few years out there."

"We need not discuss the status of her recruitment, Ryker, that conversation has been and passed. What we need to discuss is the status of her being here. Is she a disruption or not?"

Ryker shrugged, then regretted the non-committal response upon seeing Arnold's sneer.

"It's too early to tell," he said.

"How has she reacted to the child's disappearance?"

Ryker went to shrug again, then stopped himself.

"Negatively. But, as you would expect. She cared for the kid."

"Does a person like her really care for anyone?"

Ryker sighed. This was as good a time as any to bring it up. "The boy."

"The boy?"

"She cares too much for him. I don't know how we'll be about to tear him away from her."

"But I don't want him here, I just want the girl."

"I know, and I am doing all I can."

"Well, do better."

"If anything, this child's disappearance will only make her cling onto him more. Maybe his being here is something we just have to put up with."

Arnold tutted a loud tut and swiped his glare away. He leant against the fireplace and thought about the whiskey in his desk drawer.

"The boy has no function. I do not wish his presence here," Arnold said.

"Yes, but–"

"Have I made my stance on the subject perfectly clear?"

"Yes, Arnold, but it's not that simple."

"Simple? What could be simpler than a knife to his throat?"

"You want her on side do you not?"

"I want her on side, or I want her dead. At this point, either would suffice."

He walked from the fireplace to his desk and prepared his glass. He took out the whiskey and poured himself a generous portion, lifted it to his nose, smelt it, sipped it, then gulped it.

He did not offer Ryker one.

"Is she going to go hunting for this child?" Arnold asked.

"Cathryn?"

"Yes, the child."

"I—well, I don't think so."

"Think?"

"There's no way to be sure. She's unpredictable. But I don't think she'd leave the boy long enough to go search for her."

Arnold felt himself frown, highlighting wrinkles that weren't visible five or so years ago. It seemed there was always an upside and a downside to everything they did—the upside being that she would accept the child's fate, downside that she would resist the boy's.

"When is the next event?" Arnold enquired.

"Sorry?"

"You heard me. When is the next event?"

Ryker sighed, considered this; wanting his answer to be accurate.

"A week away, I think. Days, maybe."

"And we have our subjects lined up?"

"Yes."

"And this boy is a dear, dear asset to the girl."

"It would look like it."

Arnold downed the rest of his whiskey.

"Well then, I think we have another subject," he decided, and the conversation was finished, and Ryker understood.

CHAPTER FIFTEEN

AN ASSORTMENT of toy dinosaurs spread across the floor of the living room.

A living room.

An actual living room.

Cia dropped her head and covered her eyes. She sank deeper into the soft yet firm cushions of the sofa, allowing its comfort to encapsulate her in discomfort.

Boy began to rearrange the dinosaurs. He'd done this before with trees—he'd learnt all the different types of tree and could identify a tree's species and its traits in the instant he saw it. Ryker had arranged for a box of toys to be brought over, and in that box was a book about dinosaurs and a box of dinosaurs. Despite Boy being far too old for toys now, he still loved them—but not to play with them. He had simply read the book about dinosaurs and could now sort them into species and sub-species, separating them into their allocated piles.

"An Archaeopteryx," Boy muttered, "bird, flies, this goes with the Dimorphodontid and the Dsungaripterus. The

Abelisaurus, predator, theropod, that goes with another bipedal..."

Already it was giving her a headache. These facts he could remember were beyond the ability of her brain.

But she tuned it out.

Her mind still lingering on Cathryn.

It just made no sense.

Why would she run away?

Did they do something that made her runaway?

Was she still alive?

Probably not.

She felt bad for not searching for her. She wasn't sure how Ryker had convinced her not to.

Who could she have left Boy with though?

What about Dalton, he could have–

Her breath caught in her throat.

It was an unsteady relapse to two weeks ago, when she'd though she had someone she could trust.

Before he tried to...

She needed water.

She stood. Fell onto a side table, knocking Boy's glass of water to the floor.

She tried to breathe. It came out as a wheeze. A desperate surge of nothing.

"Rosy?" Boy asked.

"I'm fine," she said, though it came out as a strained whisper, like someone who had lost their voice trying to shout.

She waved her arm in an attempt to indicate that she was okay.

"Just–go back to–"

Her knees wobbled and her thighs burned and she felt so

fatigued. She collapsed onto her hands and rolled onto her back.

"Rosy?" Boy asked, approaching her.

She couldn't see him.

All she could see was Dalton.

His hands bleeding like stigmata. Holes in his palms with thick gunks of red oozing down his wrist.

"Water…" she gasped.

"Rosy?"

She rolled onto her front and tried to use her wobbling arms to push herself up.

A sudden jab in her side and Dalton was punching her there, stabbing her even, again and again, and even though he wasn't she felt the pain in her side and felt it so sharp–

"Boy… Get me water…"

Boy ran to the kitchen.

Cia rubbed her eyes and fell once again rolling seeing her father her father hands against the glass watching her run as she had trapped him in with the monsters and they devoured him they ate him tore him up spat him out a bloody mess she saw his remains and she scampered away he was nothing just inside out just torn and maimed to the soundtrack of screaming so sourly it was her fault he was dead her fault her fault her fault her fault her fault:

Her.

Fault.

"Rosy."

She looked up and Boy had a glass of water.

She tried to grab it but her hand went through it like it wasn't there and she fell onto her back and it went blank.

She was unconscious, but fully aware.

She could hear him shouting *Rosy, Rosy*, beneath the

banshee screams of the Sanctity as it collapsed and everyone died because of her and Dalton helped her escape not knowing never knowing not knowing until he's dead until he died until he killed her but he didn't she killed him she killed him she killed him she.

Killed.

Him.

Oh my God I murdered him.

I slaughtered him.

I fed him to the Masketes because I didn't have the guts to give him a quick death.

The panic ended as the storm departed and Dalton's face was all she saw.

"I trusted you," he said.

"I thought you were the one," he told her.

"I protected you," he claimed.

"No," Cia refuted. "I'm sorry. I'm sorry, Dalton, I'm sorry, so, so sorry."

"Rosy?"

Her eyes opened.

Her breathing resumed.

The ceiling spun a little, but she was aware enough to see Boy knelt over her, holding out the glass of water.

She propped herself up on her elbows, took the glass, and drank it all in one gulp.

She looked at Boy.

How could she protect him if this kept happening?

What even was it?

Boy's hand placed itself gently against her cheek, then rubbed her hair in the way she always did with him. As if mimicking her. As if doing what comforted him to comfort her.

He was intelligent.

So intelligent.

She did what she had to do to save him; she had to remember that.

Just as the surge of fear pushed itself up her gullet, she quelled the thought and returned her mind to sense.

"Let's get some fresh air," Cia said.

"Okay," Boy confirmed.

She looked at him.

So sweet. So strange. So wonderful.

She pushed herself up, found her shoes and put them on.

Her feet had felt so free without those shoes.

Together, they left the house for the sunshine, leaving a few unfinished piles of dinosaurs behind.

CHAPTER SIXTEEN

Cᴵᴬ's ʟᴇɢ strained to remained at a low pace. They felt like they should always be running.

She willed them to acclimatise, to allow her just to saunter down the street, to look at the community.

It was odd how it had lasted so long without an attack from one of the creatures.

In fact, if she listened, as much as she strained, she couldn't hear any far-off noises of screeches or growls—which was even stranger. For the past few years, she was used to always hearing something in the distance. But here, it was as if there was nothing nearby.

Which couldn't be possible.

A civilisation like this was like an all-you-can-eat buffet to one of those things.

She told herself to stop it. To be more positive.

Then she laughed at the idea.

It was her negativity, her constant wariness for what could go wrong, that had allowed them to survive. If she let that go, then...

But maybe she could let it go, sometimes. Not completely.

Just enough so she could enjoy the moment and resume her wariness whenever danger was near.

If she was going to enjoy this place, she would have to learn to relax.

"Hello there," came the northern accent of an elderly lady.

Boy had disappeared from her side and she immediately felt for the weapon hidden beneath her belt.

But it was okay.

Boy had just walked up to a lady doing some gardening.

Which was peculiar, as Boy would never approach anyone or anything without severe trepidation. For him to just walk up to a stranger...

Then again, when had he ever been able to safely approach someone he didn't know?

Maybe this place was good for him.

Maybe she should make it a home for his sake.

Maybe he could still have some resemblance of a normal adolescence—normal in the way that it used to be, that is.

"Would you like some grapes?" the woman asked.

Boy nodded eagerly.

She picked a few off a plant and handed them to him.

After living on grapes for the past few months, she'd have thought Boy would be more excited to have something else that was available—yet he seemed eager for a familiar taste.

The woman smiled at Cia.

Cia realised she was frowning and tried to smile back. She even thought about saying thank you but found it tough to form such unusual words.

Cia and Boy walked on. Boy kept rushing off to see speak to other people seeing to their fruit and vegetables, eager to see what gifts he could get.

It was a sight she never thought she'd see.

A crescendo of children's laughter caught her attention. She turned to peer into a large hall and discovered what appeared to be a classroom full of children, with the doors open to allow the sunshine in. On a board were words, with a teacher speaking each syllable slowly and particularly. The children echoed her.

They were learning to read.

As lovely as that was, Cia felt it was redundant. They should learn how to fight, how to master weapons, not how to use an ability this world no longer required.

"I know what you're thinking," came a voice beside her.

Cia turned and looked at a man, her own age, dashingly good looks. Swept back blond hair, big blue eyes, and a physique that showed he was used to manual labour.

"What?" Cia snapped.

"I said I know what you're thinking."

Cia frowned.

"You're thinking, why are they bothering to read? The world has gone to the monsters, what use is Moby Dick when they can't fight. Right?"

Cia hesitated to answer. Who was this guy?

"Let me just ask you a question," he continued. "Our community lives on, we grow in population, and we pass down knowledge of the world as it used to be. How would we do that without writing?"

"It just seems pointless."

"Knowing our history is pointless? The next generation knowing how the world used to be—is that not important?"

Cia shrugged. She did not want to admit that the guy had a point.

"I'm Hades," he said, and held out his hand.

Cia looked at it, wondering what he was doing. Then she

remembered. People used to shake hands when they met. It was something she saw her dad do a lot.

Reluctantly, she held out her hand and engaged in a handshake; something she had never experienced before.

"I didn't catch your name," Hades said.

"Cia."

"That's a nice name."

"Thanks," she said, and tried to think of what else to say. "Yours is... interesting."

"Oh yeah, my parents were deep into Greek mythology. They almost lost me when I was born, and they said I only survived because I was a fighter, so they named me Hades—after the god of the underworld. Like I was the ruler of it. Doesn't seem so great now a bunch of monsters crawled out of it."

"What?"

"Oh, didn't you know? That's where the creatures came from. Hell."

"How could you possibly know that? There's no such thing as Hell."

Hades grinned. "Tell that to the monsters."

He peered into the classroom Cia had just been peering into.

"I see you're admiring our education system. This used to be a church hall. Doesn't seem like many people want to pray anymore, so we converted it. Those that want to pray use the one on Church Street."

Yet another thing Cia found bizarre. Praying. As if a god would do this to the world then answer someone's prayer.

Cia turned to check on Boy. He sat on a bench stroking a puppy who was eager to see him, giggling as he did.

"You have pets here?" Cia said.

"Yeah, why?"

"This place, it just..."

"Seems too good to be true?"

She looked Hades up and down. Good looking, yes. Charming, absolutely. But falsely so. He had clearly spent his entire life living in fake security.

This place *was* too good to be true.

And he didn't seem to realise it.

"It just seems... I don't know..."

"I get it. You've been out there a while. You must have seen and done terrible things to survive. But this place is safe. No one will hurt you."

"Nothing like this can last. Not in this world."

"Oh, but Cia. I beg to differ. We've been standing strong since this happened."

"Exactly. No one here seems to have experienced the reality of what the world has become."

Hades smiled a sweet, sincere smile.

"Then why pity them, when you can envy them?"

She held his stare. Tried to figure him out. Tried to decide whether he was right or wrong, or whether he was neither and these were just words that meant nothing.

"I have to get back to work," Hades declared.

"What do you do?"

"I patrol," Hades said. "I keep the peace."

"Like... a policeman?"

"More like a casual security guard. It was nice meeting you, Cia."

He turned and continued to mosey up the street, smiling and saying hello to people he passed. They all seemed to know him, and he seemed to know them. A perfect world of hard workers and unmistakable safety.

She looked to Boy, throwing a ball that the puppy ran after and brought back to him.

Maybe Boy could be happy here.

Maybe they both could.

CHAPTER SEVENTEEN

THE SUN HAD MOMENTARILY HIDDEN behind the clouds as Cia and Boy returned to their new home.

Cia was shattered. She hadn't had a particularly strenuous day, but it was as if all the tension her muscles had been carrying, all the running and walking they had endured, every moment of sweat and blood and anxiety, had all accumulated and attacked her the at the first moment she'd had a day's rest. The many years of sleeping on bumps, waiting for the next attack, watching Boy's every move, had built and built and finally released itself in a burst of anguish upon her body.

"You look tired," came a voice from the house next to hers.

A man, elderly but not frail, old but not suffering, sat in a chair that he rocked ever so slightly back and forth. His face was kind and his smile was genuine.

"I am," Cia admitted. "I really am."

"Come and sit," the man said.

"I really must get back."

"I really do insist. We are going to be neighbours."

Cia paused. She looked at Boy, recognising the fatigue in him too.

"You've been through a lot," the man continued. "I can't imagine what it's like out there, and I can't imagine what it's like to adjust to life in here. Must be quite a difference."

Cia snorted an ironic snort. "You could say that."

"I wasn't here when it all first happened. I spent a year out there with my wife before they found me."

Cia was intrigued. Finally, someone who may relate to what she was trying to deal with. Not someone with this sense of perfection about them, but someone who knew what it was like to live out there then adjust to life in here.

"Rosy," Boy moaned. "I'm tired."

"Let him go to bed," the man said. "He'll be safe. I promise."

Cia was reluctant, but this man's word seemed comforting.

"Why don't you go get yourself ready for bed," Cia said. "And I'll be in soon."

"I don't want to go in alone."

Cia took his hand and squeezed it. "I won't be long."

"It'll be fine, son," the man said. "I won't keep her long."

Boy seemed to find this reassuring. He smiled at Cia and scuttled into the house.

It was tough to watch him to go and not follow. Was she being too trusting too soon?

"I'd offer you a glass of wine," the man said, "as the winemaker here is wonderful. But I imagine you've never had wine before, and I wouldn't want you to be dizzy, so there is fresh orange juice if you wish."

Fresh orange juice... Cia had forgotten such a thing existed...

"That would be perfect," she said.

She walked over and sat beside him. The seat rocked gently, and she enjoyed the motion, allowing it to relax her as much as it could.

"My name is Graham," he said.

"Cia," she answered. "Is your wife inside?"

"Pardon me?"

"You said you and your wife..."

He smiled. "My wife was gone before they brought me here."

"Oh." Cia looked down. What a stupid question.

He poured her an orange juice and handed it to her. She took a sip. It was heavenly.

"It's okay," he said. "I miss her. But, in a way, I'm glad she didn't have to experience what I experienced out there. I was pleased she was saved from it."

Cia nodded. She understood what he meant.

"What's the name of the lad with you?"

"Erm... I don't know. I call him Boy. I've never needed a name."

"Boy," he echoed. "How sweet."

"He is."

"If you ever need someone to talk to, or take care of him, I'm here. I know it's tough to trust someone after the kind of people you may have met out there, but hopefully you can learn to trust me. It gets pretty lonely up here. That house has been vacant for months."

"Months? Who was in it before then?"

He looked at her and she looked back. There was something behind his eyes, something he wanted to hide, something she knew she shouldn't have asked about.

"Not everyone can cope with this life after being out there," he said. "Sometimes it gets the better of them."

He sighed a big sigh and readjusted his position.

"But I am sure such a thing will not happen with you," he continued. "You seem strong. And you have Boy, which gives you the most important thing you need to keep living in this world."

"What's that?"

"A purpose. Imagine trying to survive out there without one."

Cia looked down at her orange juice. She drank the rest in one go.

"I should check on Boy," she said. "I don't want to leave him alone for too long."

"I understand. It was lovely to meet you, Cia."

She stood.

He held out his hand.

She shook it, and as she did, they shared a smile.

"Bye," she said, wishing she could find something more profound to depart with.

"Sleep well," he said.

She returned to the house to find Boy already asleep on the sofa. She woke him up, guided him to bed, then returned to her bedroom. Once she had checked the knife was still beneath her pillow, she fell asleep straight away.

CHAPTER EIGHTEEN

THE PEACEFUL SILENCE was still uncomfortable.

Cia lay there, on the mattress with no broken springs, listening.

Where were the growls? The screeches, the screams, the shouts?

Where was the snoring of Boy next to her?

Night time was a time for sleeping in readiness to awake at any moment. It was a time she tuned into all the sounds, from the birds in the trees to the rumbles in the distance. The passive silence unnerved her; it kept her cautious—it was odd how a group of survivors clustered into such a small area could somehow repel attacks.

A knock on the front door made her jump.

She hated that it made her jump.

It meant she was already starting to relax, to lose her alertness.

She readied her knife behind her back and made her way slowly down the stairs. She shifted the curtain of the living room and peered out.

It was that man from earlier. Hades. The god of the underworld, as he had proclaimed.

She put her knife into the back of her belt and made her way to the front door. She opened it to find him standing there, a bunch of flowers in his hand.

"Hi," he said, smiling that dashing smile again.

"Hi," Cia responded unnervingly.

"I know it's late, and I hope I didn't wake you. Is it too late?"

Cia shrugged. Too late? Another strange concept.

"Look, I am here for two things; if you want to go back to whatever you were doing, then, you know, I won't bother you. Okay?"

Cia shrugged again.

Hades presented the flowers toward her. She wasn't sure what kind they were, but she was positive Boy would know. Some of them were red, and some were yellow.

"I figured that, seeing as you have never really had the chance to date, at least I assume not, that no guy has ever brought you flowers. So I wanted to be the first."

Cia stared at them. Was she supposed to take them? He was holding them out expectantly, but she didn't know what to do.

Eventually, she took them, looked at them, and put them on the floor by her shoes.

Hades looked a little put out, but only temporarily.

"I think they left the vars in one of the kitchen cupboards."

Cia had no idea what he meant but nodded along.

"The second thing—there is a dance. For strictly eighteen to twenty-five-year-olds. Seeing as that is in our age category, and you could do with meeting people, I wondered if you would like to go with me?"

A dance?

Now this was surreal.

"It's tonight," Hades added, appearing discomforted by her lack of answer. "As in, now. But I'm sure you can find something to change into, there must be a load of dresses or something left in the wardrobe."

A dress?

Cia wasn't sure she'd ever worn a dress.

She looked up the stairs. As inviting as the thought of a dance was, she couldn't leave Boy for that long.

Besides, this guy had no idea what he'd be getting himself in to.

The last guy she kissed, she killed.

The only guy she had sex with, she murdered as he climaxed.

She dreaded to think what she would do to him. Romance wasn't really something she felt she could afford herself, or felt she deserved.

"I don't think so," she finally responded.

"Really?" he said, put out. "Because I hear they play some great music. How long's it been since you heard music?"

Cia shrugged another shrug. It was something she hadn't thought about.

"You don't have to dance, either," he persisted. "I mean, I will, and I will look like a prat doing it. You can just sit at the side and laugh if you wish."

"No. I really shouldn't."

"Shouldn't?"

Cia looked upstairs.

"He'll be fine," Hades insisted.

Cia shook her head. "Thanks for the offer."

"Well, look, if you change your mind, we're in the village

hall. If not, it would still be nice to spend some time with you on another day. It doesn't have to be dancing."

Hades reached for her hand. His thumb stroked her palm, and she flinched her hand away, protecting it against her belly.

Hades forced a smile, then turned and left.

Cia shut the door, locked it and bolted it.

Still, she watched him leave out the window, contemplating what a lovely idea going to a dance with a boy would be.

.

NOW

CHAPTER NINETEEN

CIA IS BECOMING as used to the sight of bodies as she is to the sight of trees or grass or sky. She steps over the them like it's a game of Sleeping Lions and they are all just trying to see who could stay still the longest.

She wonders if she'll recognise any faces, should they still be recognisable; though not many faces remain. She sees a few mangled features and tries to form a clearer image of what that person may have looked like.

But it is like trying to decipher a Picasso painting.

A mixture of bent noses and beaten eye sockets and missing teeth and bodies torn apart and inside out are smeared over the community.

Cia had always thought of a dead body as a blank canvas, but they aren't. Each corpse is a damaged canvas, painted with messy, obscure images.

Is this her fault?

Did she do this?

Should she just have let them...

No.

It is unthinkable.

One life for many, yes, she got it—but no.

Not that life.

Never that life.

She thinks about Boy.

Wonders if he was okay.

She wishes she could recite the poem to him right now, but she knows the words wouldn't find her lips. Besides, she would need to be beside him to do that.

There has been so much damage done.

She wonders if she should leave or hide.

But she's hidden long enough.

She wants to see this. Wants to see the wreckage.

She convinces herself it was because she feels responsible, that she wishes to take some of the blame. She even tells herself that it is her punishment to see this, that she caused it, prompted it, provoked it, and this is what she gets in return.

At one point, she even tells herself that she will cry.

But she never cries.

And that is why she really wants to see this—she is trying to feel something, willing the violence to affect her, to have the intrepid strands of guts flailing out of open chests have some lasting impact on her mental health.

But she is beyond that now.

She is blissfully numb.

These were the living, and they lost.

That is it.

Final word of their story.

The end, goodbye.

None of it means anything to anyone anymore. No one will be knocking on a family's door to let them know what happened to their loved one.

Their family was dead.

All of them dead.

It's what they deserved.

All of them, though?

Is it what all of them deserved?

Every one of them.

Each mother, each father, each son and each daughter?

Yes.

She thinks it because she wants to argue with herself; she wants another thought to chime in and tell her she is wrong, that it isn't right.

No such thought presents themselves.

It is like a walking over someone else's messy, discarded picnic. She doesn't care that it was now covered in ants.

THEN

CHAPTER TWENTY

IT FELT good to be outside the walls again. Trying to adjust to the new life in the community gave her such anxiety, and as soon as Ryker had said he and some guys were going hunting, she'd jumped at the opportunity before Ryker had finished asking the question.

Who'd have known she'd be grateful to be back in the open, around monsters again?

Her and a few guys with shotguns slung over their shoulders sauntered through the surrounding forest, looking for animals they could kill for the butcher to sort.

A few things, however, unsettled her.

Firstly, there was very little livestock still alive, and she found it unlikely they were to come across any. What's more, they were already growing livestock in the community—was there still not enough?

Secondly, these guys were walking around with heavy footsteps and loud conversations. They seemed to know nothing about avoiding the creatures whilst out here.

Thirdly, why were their guns over their shoulders? Cia's

knife was in her hands, poised and prepared, ready to use as soon as the moment called for it.

Cia paused as she heard a noise carrying along the air. The rest of the guys just walked past her, amidst conversation about their plans next day or next social gatherings or whatever things they thought about that didn't matter in this scenario.

"Wait," she said.

Ryker turned over his shoulder.

"I said wait," Cia repeated.

They stopped and turned to her, seemingly annoyed that their idle chatter was forced to cease.

She didn't care. She listened. And she heard it again.

The unmistakable squawks of many, many creatures.

"There's a Maskete nest near here," Cia said.

A few of the guys scoffed.

"What's the matter with you? They could–"

A battering of air interrupted her. She looked up to see the belly of a Maskete gliding overhead.

"Get down!" she snapped and rushed to the shelter of a log.

The others didn't get down. They just laughed.

What the hell was wrong with them?

Did they want to die?

"She for real?" one of them asked Ryker.

"Knock it off," he said.

Before Cia could confront their stupidity, the thud of a Maskete's feet shook the log she sheltered beneath.

It stood.

Metres away.

Looking them up and down.

Cia's heart raced. Her adrenaline burst through her body. She wiped sweat from her brow.

She readied her weapon.

The others just stood there. Looking at it. Like it was nothing. Like an awkward guest had just entered a dinner party.

Ignoring them, Cia stood, took aim, and readied herself for a fight.

Ryker jumped in front of her and pushed the blade aside.

"Don't," he said.

"Are you crazy?" she snapped, snatching the knife away from his hand and readying it once again.

"Cia, don't!" he insisted.

What was wrong with him?

The Maskete screeched, its voice echoing, communicating something with its nest.

Was it calling them?

Was it beckoning more?

Letting them know where the feast was?

Then something bizarre happened. Something inexplicably miraculous. Something wonderful and terrifying.

The Maskete looked upwards, took off, and flew away.

Cia looked to Ryker, then to the others.

They knew.

Somehow, they knew.

That they were safe.

That it would not attack. That it would fly away.

"What the hell is going–"

Before Cia could ask, one of the guys shouted, "Wasters!"

Now they ran. Sprinting as fast as they could, leaping over logs and ducking branches.

"Hurry," Ryker urged Cia, and she saw the fear in his face that was missing moments ago.

Over her shoulder she saw them emerge. Masses of them

from beyond the trees, shouting and jumping, surging toward them.

She tucked the knife in her belt and ran. She gained on the others quickly and ended up ahead of them; they were nowhere near as fit as her.

She glanced at Ryker as she ran, and he glanced back with a look of... she wasn't sure exactly.

Guilt?

No.

Secrecy?

Like there was something he wasn't telling her, and she was just figuring that out.

Why had the Maskete not attacked?

Why were they scared of the Wasters but not the flying monster?

The doors opened marginally for them to return into the community and shut just in time for the Wasters to be kept out.

The Wasters battered against the door, ferociously at first, then they began to grow tired.

Cia knew she was safe.

She knew they couldn't get her in there.

But there was something else she didn't know, and she was determined to find out what it was.

CHAPTER TWENTY-ONE

THE DOORS SHUT and the hunters all gave their shotguns back to the person in charge of ammunition.

Cia grabbed one of their shotguns and held it, not knowing why.

She stared at the back of Ryker's head, seething, glaring intently at the messy hair and messy lies.

"Er, Ryker," said the guy eagerly trying to take her gun from her.

Ryker paused and turned.

"What's going on?" he asked.

"She won't give me her gun," said the guy.

"Course she will."

The guy tried to take the gun again, but Cia grabbed him by the throat, squeezed, then shoved him away.

Ryker turned and strode back toward her, holding a calming hand out that did not work.

"Cia, what are you doing?"

"What is going on?" she asked, wishing her voice didn't shake so much.

"I don't know what you're asking, Cia, but why don't you

just give the gun back, then we can talk about whatever it is you–"

"I think I'll hang onto it."

Ryker exchanged a look with the person trying to take the gun. The other people who had been out hunting paused and one of them said, "Everything okay, Ryker?"

Ryker told them it was fine, to go on, he'd catch up, but their voices were all muffled like they were under water. Cia was doing all she could to keep in her rage, knowing what that rage had done, the people who had died because of it.

She wanted to fit in here, for Boy.

She wanted to make peace, for Boy.

She knew unleashing her anger and hurting people would mean they'd have to leave. She couldn't fight a whole town of people.

Or could she? They were hardly warriors.

But she was certain there was something going on, and she hated that everyone acted like life was perfect, like this was how things were now, like this was the true representation of life amidst the chaos.

"Give me the gun, Cia," Ryker said, edging closer.

"Don't come any closer," Cia demanded. The gun rattled. She wished she could calm down but didn't know how.

Flashes of Dalton screaming forced themselves back to her mind.

No, not again.

She couldn't break down.

Not now.

"Cia, please, just give him the gun and then we'll–"

"Why didn't we kill that Maskete?"

Dalton sighed.

No! *Ryker* sighed.

It was Ryker, not Dalton.

She killed Dalton.

Please don't kill Ryker…

"Cia, just give the gun–"

"Answer the question."

"We can talk about this if–"

"All right, how about a different question. Why didn't that Maskete kill *us*?"

"Cia–"

"It was next to a nest. It should have called them all to get us. But it didn't. It made a noise that told them to stop, to back off."

"Look–"

"Stop trying to calm me down!"

A few people working on crops turned to look at her.

Blobs filled her vision.

Her breath wheezed.

"You've gone red," Ryker pointed out. "Cia, for everyone's protection, we need the gun–"

"The Wasters were willing to chase us. But not the Masketes,…"

"Cia–"

"You stopped me from killing that Thoral too."

"Cia, for Christ's sake, would you just–"

"*Stop telling me to calm down!*"

She fell, her knees cutting against the gravel, her elbows pricking as they hit the surface.

The gun spun away from her and the guy picked it up but she didn't look didn't care anymore it was all just so blurry, and Dalton was there and she was stabbing him and her dad was there and he was screaming for her and everyone in the Sanctity was dead and she was fucking that guy and stabbing him as he came and watching him splurt blood out of his mouth as he shot inside of her and that is what life is now that is what life is what it–

"Get the doctor!"

Was that Ryker's voice?

She felt a hand on her back.

Was that Ryker's?

"Let's get you to the hospital wing," she heard him say.

"No!" She was not prepared to have strangers poking around at her while they sedated her. "Get me home!"

Home.

Was it her home?

That cottage would be her home.

It looked perfect until it didn't.

Until she killed Dalton in the garden.

Listened to the Masketes tear his screaming body apart as Boy comforted her.

"We really should get you–"

"No! To my bed, then—then—leave me alone!"

A gap of silence, then Dalton—no, *Ryker*—said, "Fine."

He helped her to her feet, but she became top heavy and walked back into the floor.

Oh, God, Dalton.

Dalton.

That kiss they shared, so much better than the second.

What did I do to you...

"I don't know if your home is–"

"Get me *home!*"

Her father looking at her.

Staring.

Watching as his only daughter trapped him with the monsters and watched them tear him apart.

Watched him die.

No, not just die.

Suffer in pain.

Suffer until there was no more suffering.

She brought herself to her feet again.

"Get me to my bed," she demanded, though she wasn't sure if the words came out well enough to be heard, as she fell and passed out as she was saying them.

CHAPTER TWENTY-TWO

WHEN CIA AWOKE it was still light—but that kind of amber light that only comes in a summer evening. It shone through the window in a way that made her head throb.

A glass of water sat on the cabinet beside her bed.

She took it, too thirsty to care what they have put in it, and drank it all down in one go.

She looked around.

Just as she had instructed, she was back home.

But there was a woman in there with her.

"Who are you?" she grunted.

The woman smiled as if Cia hadn't just spoken rudely.

"My name is Shan," she said, her voice as bouncy as her ponytail. "I am your nurse."

She must have been in her mid-twenties. Pretty, but not obviously so. Wearing a lab coat, as if that gave her authority.

"You took quite the fall," Shan said. "Have these episodes been happening much?"

"What episodes?"

She sat up, looked around, checking the room was the same, as if it wouldn't be.

"You collapsed after shaking and sweating. You came in and out of it, saying some strange things. Do you not know what this is?"

Cia shrugged. "Just something that happens."

"You had a panic attack, Cia," Shan said. "I imagine it's from some kind of post-traumatic stress related to your experiences out there. I assume it must have been quite upsetting."

Cia snorted.

"Quite upsetting?" She shook her head. "What is wrong with you people? Don't even know what upsetting is."

She turned and sat up.

Then she remembered the one thing she should have remembered the moment she woke up, but she'd let her defences down, let herself become too relaxed.

Boy.

She went to get up.

"I'd have some bed rest if I were you," Shan said, trying to push her back down.

Cia batted her arm away.

"You're not me."

"Really, you may have a concussion."

"I'll survive a little headache, thanks."

She pushed Shan out of the way and stood.

"At least take these pills," Shan said, taking Cia's hand and placing some pills into her palm.

"What are they?"

"Two paracetamols for the headache, and sertraline for the anxiety."

Whatever.

She swallowed them. If it got this woman out the way, then fine.

"Where's Boy?" Cia demanded.

"Excuse me?"

Cia felt a flutter of rage.

"Boy? Where is he?"

"Your friend? I believe he's next door."

Cia marched to the stairs.

"Cia," Shan called. "I'll be back to check tomorrow–"

"Don't bother."

Cia rushed out of the house. She sprinted next door, then halted, seeing that she needn't have worried.

There Graham was, sat on the porch with a glass of wine, Boy on the chair next to him rearranging his dinosaurs.

Cia halted, bending over and willing her heavy breathing to subside. She hadn't realised how much she was panting.

"Rosy!" Boy said.

She rushed over to him and stroked his hair back.

"Is everything okay?" she asked. "Are you okay?"

Boy nodded eagerly. "Graham had some more dinosaurs. Look, it's a Parasaurolophus."

Cia had no idea what that was, but she was happy Boy was happy.

She turned to Graham, who just smiled back at her.

"Thank you," she said unexpectedly.

"You're welcome," Graham replied. "We've had quite a day. He went up to see you when you were brought home, and I said I'd take care of him while you were asleep. I hope that's okay?"

Cia sat, still panting.

"Of course."

She was suddenly so grateful that she wanted to do something to show how grateful she was. She had nothing to offer however, so she made do with another, "Thank you."

"Really, you don't have to thank me."

She looked to Boy, happily turning the pages of his book to help him identify another dinosaur.

"You know," Graham said, lowering his voice so Boy didn't hear. "Before all this happened, and before I retired, I was a teacher. I specialised in helping teenagers with learning problems and worked with quite a few autistic students."

"Oh yeah?"

"If you would like me to—and, again, only if you would like me too—I'd be happy to do some work with him."

"Like what?"

"For example, teaching him how to interact with others, ways to understand and manage his anxiety, how to interact socially. Things that we all take for granted."

Cia felt like crying.

She didn't let herself, not wanting to shed any tears in front of anyone.

A surge of affection and gratitude made her want to thank him profusely—but she couldn't form the words. Maybe this place wasn't so bad.

"That would be amazing," she said, and he smiled, and they watched the sun go down together before she decided it was time for Boy to go to bed.

CHAPTER TWENTY-THREE

Seeing it was such a lovely morning, Arnold took one of his occasional forays into the community. He didn't particularly like to interact, but it was the important job of a politician to meet the people and pretend, for a short period, that you are one of them.

But he would never be one of them.

Yes, money meant little anymore—but it had already bought him enough power that these people recognised his authority.

They were all his little workers, doing his bidding, making the place function.

And all of them hoping that they weren't next for the event.

But the subjects had already been chosen, so they all scurried around with an air of relaxation that said *we are safe*.

For now.

"We need to talk," came that all-to-familiar voice from beside him. He didn't need to turn around to identify its owner. He carried on walking, his hands behind his back, strolling with stubborn authority.

"What is it?"

"It's Cia," answered Ryker.

"The girl?"

"Yes, the girl."

"What of her now?"

"She—she's asking a lot of questions."

"And?"

"And, well, I'm not sure about how to give her answers."

Arnold sighed a long, drawn-out sigh.

This was Ryker's purpose, to deal with things like this. Why must Arnold lower his hands to the mud when he should be able to just step over it?

"Maybe it's time to come clean," Ryker suggested. "Everyone else came to terms with it, eventually. They understand it's how our society survives. Maybe she would to."

"Do you believe that to be the case?"

Ryker didn't answer, but his face said all that needed to be said.

"We will have to tell her eventually," Ryker admitted. "Won't we?"

"Ryker, I leave the judgement in your hands."

"Okay, so what if I tell her, and what if she doesn't react well?"

"You know where the guns are."

"Would the people not–"

Arnold halted, turned to Ryker, and peered intently into his perplexed face.

"The people do as I damn well wish them to. This is not a democracy, this is a dictatorship, and I have dictated you to deal with the matter. If you really can't do it yourself, get someone to do it for you. Get her to see Christoph, he is well-trained in developing trust with reprobates. Use him."

Ryker nodded. Another problem solved by Arnold that should have solved by someone else.

He contemplated walking through more of the community, but it was hot, and he'd had enough. The whiskey was waiting for him, as was a nice fan that would keep him cool.

"There's another thing," Ryker said.

"What now?" snapped Arnold.

"There were some Wasters. They seemed angry; we don't know what they will do."

"Well then, I will be sure to lock my doors tonight, and you will be sure to have the relevant people on standby."

Ryker nodded. "Right you are."

Arnold faked a smile and turned back to his office, where he wouldn't have to face any more of these pointless conversations.

CHAPTER TWENTY-FOUR

CIA NEVER SLEPT HEAVILY. Even now, as she lay in a snug bed in a safe home, a simple bird call or someone shuffling past in the street below would momentarily stir her from her sleep. She wasn't always consciously aware of it, but her body was poised, ready for trouble.

So one can imagine how quickly she leapt from her bed when an ear-piercing scream startled her awake.

She stumbled to the floor, from deeply asleep to urgently alert in seconds. She made her way to the window, opened the curtains, and looked to the ground below.

She registered the sound of more screams before she registered the blood. A woman lay on her back while something fed on her guts, pulling them out and forcing her to watch her own agony before she died.

It was a Waster.

She looked across the street to the entrance, where the doors were marginally open, possibly having welcomed someone back from hunting or whatever they may have been doing—only to have Wasters force their way in.

There was more than just one, or two, or three even.

There were a dozen. Maybe even a few dozen. All bursting in and spreading like water breaking down a dam.

She looked back to the one feeding on a dying woman below her; the woman of which, it appeared, had finally finished dying.

The Waster feeding on her body paused.

Looked up at Cia.

They locked eye contact.

The moment their eyes met she knew it was a mistake.

It ran toward their home. It left her sight, but she didn't need to see it to know where it was; the house shook as it threw its body repeatedly against the front door.

The door wouldn't hold for long.

Just as she went to retract back into her room, she noticed another Waster doing the same to the house next to hers.

Graham...

Her priority was Boy.

Then she would help Graham.

She sprinted from her room to his, every thud prompting another pulse of her headache.

"Boy!" she shouted, but he was already awake, and he was already covering his ears and shaking his head.

She grabbed his arms, and he tried to continue shutting the world out, but she didn't have time, so she pulled him from his bed.

"Help me," she instructed, taking one end of the bed and pulling it.

He just looked at her quizzically.

"Do it!"

Reluctantly, and much to Cia's appreciation, he chose not to argue. He helped Cia pull the bed up to the door.

Cia paused when it was a step away and opened the wardrobe door.

"When I leave this room, I need you to do two things for me, do you understand?"

He looked alarmed. She could see him processing fear, could see him realising this was the voice she only used when they were in danger. If she could talk to him quickly enough, she could hopefully get through to him before he broke down.

"Answer me!"

He nodded.

"Push the bed against the wall, then get into the wardrobe, and do not open the wardrobe door until you hear me calling. Do you understand?"

He nodded.

"Repeat it to me."

"Push the bed against the door," he replied, rubbing sleep out of his eyes. "Get in the wardrobe. But why?"

"Do you trust me?"

He nodded.

"Then you will do it. And when you push, push with all your might. Okay?"

He nodded.

Downstairs, she heard the front door thwack against the inside wall.

The Waster was in.

She stepped outside the room and closed the door. She waited a moment to listen to him moving the bed, so she knew he was carrying out her instructions. Then, she left his room, fetched a chair, and slammed it down upon the door handle.

It did nothing.

This did not deter her. Powered by the extra strength adrenaline afforded her, she continued to batter against the door handle with the chair, again and again and again, until eventually, after numerous strikes, the door handle struck off.

She retreated to her bedroom, to her pillow, and took the knife from beneath it. She kept the door to her room open but hid behind it.

Thuds rose up the stairs and paused at the top of it. Its sniffing was even louder than its panting breath. It sniffed harder and harder, enjoying the potent smell of a fresh young lady.

Her fingers flexed around the handle of the knife.

She closed her eyes and listened to the sounds, imagining its corresponding movements.

It shambled forward in sudden bursts of heavy steps. It paused outside Boy's room and she had to remind herself she'd taken the handle off and he'd blocked the door; as long as the Waster didn't know Boy was in there, he was fine.

It moved on and came closer.

She could smell its body odour, the stench of which was in such stark contrast to the fresh lavender sheets she had been sleeping in only minutes ago.

It stepped into her room and she watched its silhouette from the crack between the door and the wall.

She lifted the knife, waiting for the opportune moment.

It sniffed—one large intake of ecstasy. It held its breath, enjoying the sumptuous scent, and stepped forward.

Cia launched herself across, lunging the knife toward it.

She scraped the side of its neck, causing it to stumble but little else.

Knowing its strength outdid hers, its power, its killer instincts, all being superior, she did not let up—she pushed the knife forward once more, stabbing its throat, which seemed to make it stumble.

But it's never easy to cut someone's throat. It isn't like the movies her dad never let her watch where you give one strike and blood bursts everywhere; especially with the small

WHEN THE LIVING HAVE LOST

muscles of her bony arms. It takes more attempts, and more strength.

So she struck more.

Again and again and again until she no longer blinked at the blood splatters flashing against her face.

Until the Waster was an empty body with multiple wounds to its throat.

She didn't wait to see if sprung back up or check to see if it had a pulse. She ran from the room to the hallway, checking the door to Boy's room was still immovable.

Her next thoughts were to Graham.

The kind old man willing to help Boy.

The man she could relate to.

She burst down the stairs, and into the street, entering the chaos outside.

CHAPTER TWENTY-FIVE

Cia recalled the flash of a memory. Years ago, when the creatures rose, and the streets were full of screaming. When no one knew what to do and everyone was running and screaming and helpless. A painting of chaos.

They were so unprepared for this.

Everyone was screaming—which would only attract the Wasters more. In fact, from her experience of Wasters, they would find this all the more arousing.

No one fought them.

No one even tried.

Well, they'd asked her to be a warrior.

And this was what they'd asked her to be a warrior for; because she was the only one here who knew how to survive.

She ignored the frenzied scene, neglected the anarchy, and made her way to Graham's house. Something already battered the door down.

As she entered, she heard a gunshot.

She sprinted up the stairs and skidded into a room where Graham quickly turned the barrel of his gun toward her.

"It's me!" she shouted.

Graham abruptly stopped and lowered the gun to his side. Across the room was a dead Waster with half its face missing.

"Are you all right?" Graham asked.

"Yeah," she replied. "I'm fine."

"Boy?"

"He's safe. He's locked in a wardrobe; they can't get to him."

"Good. Let's hide."

Graham began limping down the corridor.

Why was he limping?

She noticed blood trailing from his leg.

Cia didn't follow.

"Are you coming?"

She shook her head.

"Don't be a fool," Graham said.

"They brought me here to be a warrior."

"There are no warriors. They will kill you."

"Because I'm a girl?"

Graham smiled gracefully. "Not at all. Because they are Wasters."

She looked at his leg, of which he was putting less and less pressure on.

"Get a bandage around that," she said. "But first, tell me how to use your gun."

"Cia, I don't think–"

"You've been out there, and you've been in here. You know how defenceless these people are. They will kill everyone then they search for the hidden survivors including–"

She stopped herself from saying Boy. She couldn't admit to him being in potential danger again.

"I'll come with you," Graham decided.

"Look at your leg. You'll slow me down. Just give me the gun and show me how to load it."

It was a simple hunting weapon, one that took four bullets at a time. He told her the gun's name, but she didn't both to remember it. It wasn't information that mattered. She'd always relied on knives and hands, as guns could run out of ammunition where knives couldn't; now, however, was a good time for a crash course.

He handed it to her and shut himself in the bathroom. It was heavier than she expected, but she lifted it and carried it all the same.

She tried to shoot at a Waster as soon as she left the house, but the bullet went into the sky as the kickback hurt her shoulder.

The sound distracted the Waster, and it came hurtling toward her.

She tried to shoot it again, but the same thing happened. She discarded the gun into Graham's house, shut the door, and readied her knife.

She ducked its attempt to grab her and swung the knife upwards, slicing it beneath the chin. She swung again, forcing the knife further in. It took a lot of strength to pull it back out again, but when she did, the Waster seemed to fall into a pool of its own blood.

Another Waster chased a woman who held her toddler across her chest.

Cia gave chase but couldn't keep up.

"Hey!" she shouted, and caught its attention, allowing the woman to escape.

But she also caught the attention of another Waster behind her, and another to her side.

"Shit," she muttered.

She did not know how to get out of this one.

But, as soon as the worries came, a stream of bullets bombarded the Waster's heads and bodies and they each fell down dead.

Behind her was Ryker, along with a few of the guys who went hunting earlier, and a few others she hadn't met, all with their guns.

"Come on," Ryker said, and she followed, feeling useless now they were all here with their semi-automatics.

She ended up trailing behind and checking on the victims. It didn't take long before their guns had disposed of the rest of the Wasters.

Cia waited for the chaos the gunshots would attract, for the stampeding Thoral or screeching Maskete or hissing Lisker to burst into the community.

Just an eerie silence responded.

"Everyone spread out and check there's none left."

They all went off on their own, taking their allocated areas of the town and checking every home, every building, every street, ensuring there were no more Wasters lurking anywhere.

By the time they reconvened, Cia was burning with questions.

"I need answers," she told Ryker.

"Right now we need to–"

"You do whatever you need to do. You obviously will not tell me. I'm going to see Arnold."

He went to stop her, but the wail of a man on the floor caught his attention. The doctors and nurses came onto the scene, seeking reassurance that it was safe for them to attend to the victims.

Cia left them behind and marched to Arnold's lavish

office. The place where Arnold was safe and secure, one of the few buildings with no decorations of violence, hidden away from any pain—as a true politician would be.

CHAPTER TWENTY-SIX

CIA KICKED THE DOOR, expecting it to burst open.

It did not.

So she battered and hammered and pushed and shoved and shouted but the door would not buckle.

Ryker appeared behind her.

"He's not going to let you in while you try to barge it down," Ryker said. "He'll think you're a Waster."

She ignored him.

She pulled on the handle and kicked and shoved at it, shouting obscenely about how Arnold better open up.

Ryker stepped forward.

"Allow me," he said, and tapped lightly on the door.

A few footsteps came from behind it, and it cautiously opened.

"Ryker?" said Arnold.

"Cia has some questions she wants to–"

Cia knocked the door open, ignoring the pain it caused her shoulder. She entered the office and stood in the centre, looking around at the lavish architecture, the pristine surfaces, the expensive booze.

"So this is where you are?" Cia asked.

Arnold glanced at Ryker and they exchanged a look, as if something unsaid passed between them, and the secrecy only infuriated Cia more. Then Arnold turned to her and smiled warmly, which infuriated her once again.

"Please, sit," he said, indicating the leather sofa behind her.

"I'd rather stand," she said.

"As you wish."

Arnold walked over to his desk, brushed a few invisible specs off the edge, and leant against it. Ryker walked in, past Cia, and to the window where he looked out, then leant against the windowsill.

Cia looked between them. Both of them looked to her expectantly, as if she was the one who needed to give answers.

"Your people are dying," Cia said. "Being slaughtered by Wasters. And you're up here with a locked door and a whiskey to accompany the entertainment."

"I assure you I am most regretful that–"

"Fuck off," Cia snapped. "Don't talk to me like a politician. All politicians are dead. I saw them die."

"You saw what?" Ryker interrupted, and Cia realised she had said too much. She had forgotten that she had things to hide too.

"I imagine," Arnold said, ignoring the outburst, "that you assume I should be down there, dying with them, yes?"

"Fighting with them," Cia corrected.

"And I cannot fight, so I would die. That's what you want?"

"You seem to rationalise a lot of things with this theory that because other people suffer it doesn't mean you should. It's nice; it means you can forget about everyone else."

"I do not forget about everyone else," Arnold said, a touch of anger flinching his smile. "I bought this town to save as many as I could, and I damn well did that. I did my part, young lady."

"Young lady?"

Cia felt her fingernails digging into her palm.

Young lady?

It caused her the biggest rush of aggression yet. To insinuate that because she was young, and because she was a lady, it allowed him to condescend to her...

He had no idea who she was and what she was capable of.

"If you have questions," Ryker stepped in. "Then why don't you just ask them?"

"Fine. Why did no one kill the Maskete earlier?"

"Because Arnold told us not to," Ryker interjected, despite Cia looking at Arnold and vehemently addressing her questions to him.

"Okay. Why did the Maskete not kill us?"

"Because it didn't want to."

"Then why did the Wasters attack?"

Ryker shrugged. "Jealousy."

"Jealousy?"

"Exactly."

"Jealous of what?"

"Us."

"Why?"

"Because they don't like that the creatures let us–"

"Enough!" Arnold interrupted. "Go to bed. We have a clean-up crew who will sort out the street and the bodies. When you wake up, this will all be done."

"And forgotten about? Like everyone else who died?"

"Grow up," Arnold said, his patience beginning to subside, Cia just starting to see the man behind the words.

"What are they jealous of?" Cia asked defiantly.

No one said anything.

"Tell me what they are jealous of."

"Us," Arnold said resolutely. "Because the creatures let us live."

"Why do they let you live? They are mindless animals with no conscious knowledge of who they should or shouldn't kill."

"You think you know them better than us?" Arnold surmised. "Well, you have just demonstrated with your lack of knowledge about these creatures how little you actually know. You know of their killing, you know of being chased, of having to hide—you do not know of the other side to the creatures. The side that does have conscious knowledge. The side where they are not mindless animals."

"Are you saying they are intelligent beings?"

"It would be foolish not to think that."

"And so why do they decide not to attack us? And why don't the Wasters like that?"

Arnold stood. Sighed. Moved to the chair behind his desk and sat. Removed a cigar from his draw and smelt it.

"Ryker," he said, not looking up at Cia. "Please escort Cia back to her house. I will not be answering any more questions tonight."

Ryker walked up to Cia.

"You put a fucking hand on me and I'll rip it off," she snapped.

"You have a lot of gumption," Arnold concluded. "But if you do not acquiesce to Ryker's request for you to remove yourself from my chambers, then we have more people who will remove you and your child from the town completely. Which I do not want to do. I like you, Cia. But it is time to go, so do so."

With a final glare, she reminded herself she needed to think of Boy, and she allowed Ryker to escort her out.

CHAPTER TWENTY-SEVEN

By the time Cia had returned, Boy was asleep. She'd used a crowbar Ryker had graciously agreed to acquire for her to lever open his bedroom door, then retrieved him from the wardrobe. She had momentarily awoken him to guide him to bed, where she had left him.

She would speak to someone the next day about getting a new door put in.

For now, she lay in her bed, staring at the ceiling, wishing she would sleep.

They had a clean-up crew, as Arnold had said. When she woke up the bodies would be gone, and the blood would be cleaned. People would go about their normal business like nothing happened.

It was no better than the sanctity.

Except these people hadn't excluded her like the sanctity had. They had taken her in. Given her and Boy a home.

Should she respect that?

Eventually, her eyes closed, and she left this world for another where her problems were far away in the distance.

Then she heard it.

A groan of the floorboard outside in the hallway.

A creak of her bedroom door opening.

That same sniff of the Waster, trying to find her. She hid herself beneath the covers, not wanting to fight anymore, wanting to bury herself away like Boy did and pretend that it wasn't happening.

If she shut it out, drowned out the sniffing and the creeping, then maybe, just maybe, it wasn't really there.

But she could smell it getting closer.

Creeping forward.

Until she could make out its vile figure through the duvet, a silhouette standing over her, reaching out its hand, its long, sharp, yellow fingernails ready to scrape across her neck.

It would feed on her.

It would tear her apart.

It would fuck her entrails.

Because that's what it was. A disgusting, foul beast, incapable of human emotion, because it had sacrificed what it once was to be a slave.

It was once a man. With a wife, kids, maybe even a dog.

A job.

Parents.

Friends.

Now was a mindless cannibalistic beast.

It peeled back her duvet. A gunk of saliva dropped onto her forehead and bled down her cheek.

She couldn't hide.

She had to fight.

She shoved the duvet down, swiped the knife from beneath her pillow and held it out to its neck.

Her eyes opened, and she awoke.

She was perspiring so hard beads of sweat dripped into her eye and stung until she blinked it out.

She was holding her knife.

Panting.

But no one was there.

Sunshine came through the window. It was morning.

Outside she could already hear the regular hustle and bustle of civilians carrying out their jobs.

She was alone.

There was no Waster.

There never was.

NOW

CHAPTER TWENTY-EIGHT

I DID IT AGAIN, she says.

History has repeated itself, she gasps.

How could I have let myself... she muses.

But no one hears her.

Because she says nothing. With no one around to hear them, the words do not exist.

At this precise moment, nothing exists but her.

She looks up to Arnold's window, to the chambers, expecting him to be looking down at her.

But no one looks down at her.

All the people are below her, but none of them look up at her either.

Saying that, most of the eyes that remain are open. Their deaths were so quick or painful or graphic they didn't even have a chance to close them. They were forced to watch as the creature removed every part of them.

She wonders whether they understood what was happening, whether they felt the pain or if their minds and bodies were just numb by then.

Then she realises it didn't matter.

She is alone and never has she felt it more.

Not when she killed her dad.

Not when she killed Dalton.

And now, when there is no one by her side.

Not even Boy.

She has no one to protect, and no one to save her.

She has no reason or cause or anything.

She bows her head and closes her eyes.

She can still smell it. She can shut it out behind her eyelids, but it still invades her other senses. The overwhelming silence and the potent odour of death.

All the creatures are gone now.

There is no one left to take her.

How she wishes there was.

How she wishes she could give herself the instant relief of a brief, painless, undignified death.

What is the point of going on in this world?

There is nothing to work toward. No career or partner or home to protect. Just surviving and surviving and surviving—but for what?

What is the point of surviving just for survival's sake?

She sees something twitch. A body, twenty or so feet away from her. A child. A boy. His open chest moving.

She does not wait. She runs—maybe this one needn't die because of her. Maybe no one else need die because of her.

She lands by the boy's side, scraping her knees on the gravel. His eyes are empty and his mouth not moving. He is pale, stiffened as if dead, but the slit in his chest is throbbing.

Was it his heart trying to beat?

His lungs trying to breathe?

She places her hands either side of the open wound and moves it open to look.

Something bursts out at her and squeaks. She leaps back, and a rat runs across the street.

The boy stops throbbing now the rat is gone.

There is something still living, but not this kid.

Across from them, his mother still stares at her.

"I'm sorry," Cia tells her.

The mother says nothing. Just continues to stare. She can't figure out where the rest of this woman's body is, but it doesn't matter. It is her eyes that judge her.

"Fuck off," she tells her.

Why should she be sorry?

She didn't do this.

She bows her head.

"I'm sorry," she said.

She shouldn't have snapped.

She did do this.

Again.

Over and over again.

THEN

CHAPTER TWENTY-NINE

DAYS WENT BY, and so did weeks. Cia and Ryker left each other alone, and she didn't see much of Arnold. It seemed as if they were content pretending the other didn't exist.

Cia was up early most mornings. She kept waking up, startled and ready for a fight that wasn't there. In the end, she would give up getting any more sleep and drag herself out of bed. She would be tired, but it meant she could witness the sunrise from the garden window; prompting thoughts of how much she missed the sight of the distant amber glow rising in on the horizon.

Seeing the sunrise and sunset had always been an omen for another day of struggling or a night of worrying. It was so nice to watch it and feel safe, knowing that it was not announcing another day of pure survival. The Waster attack was a while ago and, despite her terrible night's sleep, she felt safe—something that both concerned her and pleased her.

She had just finished her second coffee when Boy emerged into the kitchen.

"Morning," Cia said.

She didn't realise she was smiling. Boy's face lit up to see her happy. It wasn't something he was used to.

"What would you like for breakfast?" Cia asked, bringing the various cereal boxes out of the cupboard. Boy pointed to the one he wanted, and she gave him a bowl and some milk.

Cereal. Bowl. Milk.

She shook her head in disbelief.

It no longer felt unsettling to have such luxuries—it felt satisfying.

Maybe they deserved this life.

A knock on the door caught her attention. She gave Boy another smile and went to see who it was.

"Hey," Ryker said as she opened the door.

"Hi," Cia said.

"I just wanted to come along and... apologise, I guess."

"What for?"

"I know we left things badly after the Waster attack."

"Okay."

"I mean, we know you have questions. But, same as you need to take your time to trust us, we need to take our time to trust you."

"So there are answers you can give me?"

"In time. We will be honest with you; you'll learn what you need to learn. But, please, be patient."

She guessed that was fair. Trust went both ways. If she took a moment to stop being so hostile, she would realise that.

"Fine," she concluded.

"There was one more thing," Ryker added.

"Yes?"

"We have a therapist here."

Cia awaited further explanation. When none was coming, she said, "And...?"

"And I really think he could help you."

"Hah!" Cia couldn't help a little outburst of laughter. "You are kidding, right?"

"I'm thinking about how you collapsed. We thought you were ill, but Shan said it was a panic attack."

"I'm not going to go open up to some therapist, Ryker."

"All I'm asking is you try him. One session. You're clearly struggling with some kind of anxiety, and I think he could help, really."

"I don't think—"

"What good are you going to be for us out there if you collapse under your own stress? It will make you a better warrior."

Cia hesitated. She sighed.

A few days ago, just the idea of it would prompt her to get violent and start screaming and attacking and—

That wouldn't be a healthy reaction.

But a therapist?

Please.

She erred and ahed, going back and forth between abhorrent rejection and optimistic willingness.

"Just one session," Ryker said. "If you don't like it, don't go again."

Cia exhaled. Maybe she needed some help readjusting to a 'normal' life. It was still something she was not used to.

"Fine," she said, and immediately regretted it. Ryker gave her the details and left before she changed her mind.

An hour later, dressed and full on sugary cereal, she took Boy next door to Graham, who was so pleased to see him. Graham really seemed to know how to interact with him, and how to look after him. Maybe Cia was even beginning to trust him.

She followed the directions Ryker had given her. She turned left at the end of the street, then right a little further on, and after ten minutes of walking, she reached it. A small cottage with a plaque on the door reading *Christoph Jason P.H.D, therapist.*

She went to turn back.

This was ridiculous.

How could she even—

Before she could completely change her mind, the door opened, and there stood a man who looked like a poor imitation of Sigmund Freud. A white beard, white hair, tweed jacket, beige trousers, checked shirt.

"You must be Cia," he said. His voice was quiet and kind, in a way that Cia could never imagine being nasty.

"Yeah, I was just…"

What? Just what?

"You're a little hesitant, aren't you?" Christoph observed.

"Yeah. I don't really know… I mean… I don't think…"

"Tell you what. Why don't we just start with a cup of tea?"

A cup of tea.

She could do that.

She followed him into a kitchen where he boiled the kettle and placed tea bags into two separate cups.

Cia watched him, expecting conversation; anticipating questions and small talk. Yet Christoph remained quiet. In fact, he didn't even look at her.

Was this a classic therapist technique? Just wait for the patient to talk, don't fill the silences?

"How do you take it?" Christoph asked.

"Er…"

"The tea?"

"Oh. Just milk, I guess."

She couldn't remember any other way of taking it.

Christoph made the tea and handed a mug to Cia.

"Shall we?" he said, and walked through to his office, Cia following.

It was quite a small room. There was no long couch for her to lie on and no Rorschach tests for her to interpret as blood splatters or dead bodies. There was just a desk, with a chair beside it that Christoph sat on, and a comfy, cushioned chair opposite for Cia.

"How are you settling in?" Christoph asked as they sat down.

"Erm... okay."

"Just okay?"

"Well, it's strange, isn't it?"

"How so?"

"It's not... I guess, it sounds weird to say, but it's not real. It's just made up. This is fiction, out there is the real world."

"Is that so?"

She was confused.

"What do you mean?" she asked.

"What makes you think the world in here is fiction, and the world out there real. Maybe it could be the other way around?"

Cia didn't know what to say. She hadn't thought of it that way.

"I guess places like this don't really exist anymore."

"If they don't exist, then how are you here?"

"I mean, I can't see another place like this being real."

"Why not?"

"Because the creatures wouldn't allow it. They'd tear it apart."

"It sounds a little like you want them to tear it apart. As if it would prove you right to have this community collapse; so you can stand there and say I told you so."

Cia frowned.

"I don't want this community to collapse, not at all."

"Then why are you so desperate for it to be fake?"

"Because—I just got so used to running and fighting. I don't even know what to do with myself anymore."

Woah.

She paused.

Took a mental step back.

She didn't even know that about herself. How had she admitted something so personal, so soon, that she hadn't even known of?

This guy was good—and suddenly that made her feel exceedingly uncomfortable.

"Are you okay?" he asked.

"Yes."

"You're fidgeting."

"Am I?"

"Does it make you uncomfortable to talk about what you've been through?"

She shrugged. "I just don't see what talking about it would do. I don't want to have to relive it."

"But you are reliving it, aren't you? Involuntarily? You keep on having these episodes where you see things you've done, things that have been done to you. Do you not?"

Cia didn't know what to say. She just vaguely nodded.

"What you are suffering from, Cia, is post-traumatic stress disorder. It means you have suffered a lot of torment, a lot of violence, and you are struggling to get past it."

"I don't want to get past it."

"Why not?"

"Because it's part of what helped me to survive."

"And is it still helping you survive? Or is it making you suffer?"

Cia exhaled. Looked at her feet.

"I have to protect Boy, whatever happens."

"And there it is."

"What?"

"The reason you can't let it go. Your love for Boy is both your greatest weakness, and your greatest strength."

"I'm not going to stop loving him."

"Of course not. But do you not want him to be happy?"

Cia peered at Christoph. Would letting go of what she'd done, what she'd seen, really be the way to make Boy happy?

She'd been so set on helping him survive, she'd never considered how to make him content.

Of course, she'd do what she could to help him smile, help his morale—because that's what stopped him from breaking down, and helped them keep moving when creatures were near.

"What exactly should I do then?" she asked.

"Face these memories you keep trying to bury or run from. Face them and accept them."

"Accept what I've done?"

"Accept what you *had* to do."

"But... if I hadn't... then..."

"Then you wouldn't be alive, and neither would Boy. You have a right to be happy, Cia. And this is your opportunity."

She had a right to be happy?

She hadn't even thought...

She wiped her eyes on her sleeve, unaware that she was crying. She hated herself for it. It was a weakness.

And, just as she thought it a weakness, she realised how much she needed his help.

CHAPTER THIRTY

THE EARLY EVENING coolness helped to calm Cia and allow her to reflect on that day's meeting.

She'd just accepted being messed up as a vital part of survival. Perhaps she hadn't realised how much of a mental strain everything she had done put on her.

The only problem was, as much as she knew sharing the things she'd done might help—she could not let anyone here know all of the atrocities she'd committed. These people would be far too naïve to understand.

Graham sat at a table with Boy, who was eagerly engaged in their activity. Cia was always astounded how keen he was to learn. She assumed he'd be too anxious to try something that he would find difficult—yet here he was, sat beside Graham, doing all he could.

"And this one," Graham said, holding up a picture of a man with an large frown. "What can you tell me about this person?"

"He's upset."

"What kind of upset?"

Boy looked puzzled.

"Is he sad upset, lost upset..."

"Angry upset."

"Yes, he definitely is, isn't he?"

Boy smiled.

"And how can we tell that he's angry upset?"

Boy studied the picture a little more. Cia could see how difficult it was for him, but he tried.

"Because his mouth is curved down," he answered.

"Yes, well done! What else?"

"His eyebrows are kind of pointed inwards."

"They are, aren't they?"

"And he looks like he's sweating."

"Very good. It's a definite frown, isn't it?"

Boy nodded.

"And what would we do if we saw a person with this expression?" Graham asked.

Boy thought about this.

"Run?" he suggested.

"Maybe. Maybe. Is there anything else we could do?"

"Ask him why he's angry?"

"We could do. Anything else?"

"Leave him alone to calm down."

"All very good suggestions!"

Cia could tell that Graham was once a great teacher. He was so enthusiastic and so engaging. It was exactly what Boy needed.

"And what about this person?" Graham asked, lifting a card. "Now this one's a little more difficult, so take your time."

Boy studied it. It was a woman winking obviously, slanting her head with an open mouth to stress the gesture.

"She's got one eye closed," Boy observed.

"She has. And do you know what that is called?"

Boy shook his head.

"It's called a wink. Do you know what a wink is?"

Boy shook his head again.

"It's when you close one eye and direct it at someone. Like this."

Graham winked obviously, which made Boy chuckle.

"What do you think the person means when they wink?"

Boy thought about this. He studied the picture.

"That they like you?"

"It could do, it could do. But maybe it could mean something even deeper than that."

"Like what?"

"It could mean, for example... I trust you. Do you know what trust means?"

Boy nodded. "It's when you rely on someone and believe them."

"Precisely! And a wink is like, hey, you, we trust each other. We're all right."

Boy smiled.

"Can you try a wink?"

Boy tried to wink but ended up moving his whole head to the side and blinking both eyes. Graham and Cia chuckled, and Boy joined in.

"You'll get there eventually," Graham said, placing the cards down. "I think that's enough for today. What do you think?" he asked Cia.

"I think Boy has done really well and worked really hard. I would agree."

Boy beamed with pride.

"Why don't you go get ready for bed and I'll be there in a minute."

Boy nodded and stood.

"What do you say to Graham?"

"Er..."

Cia called Boy over and whispered in his ear. He turned to Graham and said quietly, "Thank you."

"You're welcome," Graham said.

Boy ran across to the house next door and disappeared inside.

"Thank you so much for this," Cia said. "He's learning so much, it's really helping him. I'd never even have even thought of doing something like this."

"It's no problem, really. It's made me realise how much I miss it; it's been so long."

Cia stood.

"He's an extraordinary boy," Graham said. "And that's a credit to you. You've taken good care of him."

There were hundreds of ways she could have responded to such a nice, unexpected compliment; from extreme gratitude to constant tears.

As it was, she replied with, "Good night," and left for her own home, thinking about what Graham had just said.

CHAPTER THIRTY-ONE

A FEW MORE WEEKS PAST where Graham continued to teach Boy, and Cia continued to quell her wariness. Relaxation still seemed to be her enemy but, slowly, she was overcoming her reservations.

This place was beginning to feel like home.

Having learned that there was a gym, Cia decided to try it out. It could be good for her to work out some of her aggression and frustration by punching a punching bag or doing some running.

A gym was another thing that seemed a bizarre concept—but those bizarre concepts were her reality now, and she was just about starting to accept that.

Boy came with her, not wanting to be alone. As soon as they entered, he ran to a chair and covered his face with his book about dinosaurs. He sat there, engrossed, muttering names and facts to himself, oblivious to the world around him.

Cia looked down at what she was wearing, appreciative of the clothes that had been leant to her but feeling uncomfortable in them. Leggings and a sports bra. It was so different to the comfortably ripped and torn clothes she had become accustomed to—but, again, trying to adjust and all that.

She found the corner where the punching bag was. She walked past a few guys huffing as they lifted weights in sweat-coated vests, and a woman lunging forward with her hair tied back and make up perfectly applied.

Make up.

Who had decided that people still needed makeup after the end of the world?

Luckily, Cia was away from everyone else, meaning she wouldn't be bothered and no one could stare at her—she hoped, anyway. She lunged into the punching bag with one fist, surprised by its resistance. She thought she had quite a good punch, but that was probably how it was designed; to be a challenge.

After a few more swings forced the bag to sway, she realised she had been tuning out a crescendo of huffs and smacks from an adjacent room.

She leant back to peer in and did a double take.

Wandering away from the punching bag, she moved into the other room and hovered by the door.

There was Arnold and Ryker. In a boxing ring. Arnold in vest and shorts that revealed his age and his bony physique, against a more muscular Ryker, topless and sweaty. Sparing. Throwing punches back and forth, ducking and dodging and congratulating the other for landing a blow every now and then.

"Let's pause there," said Arnold, his voice too posh to seem right in a boxing ring. "It appears we have a visitor."

They both stopped and looked at Cia.

"I'm sorry, I—I just heard, and I—"

"Oh, it's all right. A man of my age struggling away in

such a situation must be quite the sight. I would stand and gawk as well."

"I wasn't... I mean, I didn't mean to..."

"Hey, Little Miss Tough Girl," Ryker said. "Why don't you come in and do a bit of sparing with me?"

What? Sparing?

As in, fighting for pleasure, not survival?

Cia didn't jump at the opportunity.

"Come on," Ryker insisted. "You say you're all toughened up from being out there, that we are all unprepared in here. Well come on, let me see what you got."

Cia hesitated. She knew she was being baited, and she did not want to fall for it. At the same time, he was demeaning her and her experiences and that infuriated her.

"Oh, go on," Arnold said, leaving the ring and wiping his brow with a towel. "It's harmless fun."

Cia huffed. "Fine."

She stepped into the ring and faced Ryker.

"Let's see your stance then," he said.

He lifted his fists into a guard in front of his face.

She shrugged. She'd never taken a starting position before. Normally the fight finds her before it's too late.

Still, she mimicked his stance.

Ryker began circling her, and she circled back. They paced around the ring, Ryker looking into her eyes, dodging his head from one side of his fists to the other, Cia wondering what exactly she was meant to be doing.

He charged forward, went to strike, and she ducked, backed away, and ended up on the ropes.

He backed off.

"What's the matter?" he asked with an expression that made her feel stupid and humiliated.

"Nothing," she said, feeling her anger rise. "Let's do this."

She stepped forward, and this time she went to strike—throwing a punch, which he sidestepped, then another, and another, before he swiped his foot and took her out by the ankles.

"Woah, I thought it was just punches," she said, pushing herself back to her feet.

He shrugged. "It's whatever you want it to be."

Wrath rose through her body. She stood, clenched her fists, and unknowingly snarled.

"Just so you know," he said, leering at her, "I'm holding back. Seeing as you're a *girl*."

Now this pissed her off.

"Well, don't," she spat spitefully.

He shrugged. "As you wish."

She lurched forward and went to strike. The next thing she knew, she was on her knees, clutching a cheek bone that throbbed and throbbed against her hand.

She looked up at Ryker, scowling.

"You told me not to hold back," he said.

She went to get up and charge at him again, but was halted by the only sound that seemed to calm her.

"Rosy!"

Boy came rushing into the ring and to her side, wrapping his arms around her.

"Rosy, are you okay?"

She looked at Boy.

Boy, who probably couldn't understand why they were punching each other.

"I'm fine," she told him, and let him guide her out, deciding to leave the gym for another day.

CHAPTER THIRTY-TWO

"LET'S TALK ABOUT LOVE," said Christoph, as if beginning some cheesy song from a time long forgotten.

"Love?" replied Cia.

"Yes. Love. Who do you love?"

"Well, Boy. Of course. That's it."

"Yes, but that is more of a paternal love. I am talking about a fiery love."

"Fiery?"

"Romantic, if you will."

Cia shifted. She straightened her sleeves and readjusted her seat.

"There is no romantic love," she asserted.

"Within the many years you have spent out there, have you never come across someone you cared for?"

She looked at him and his piercing blue eyes. It was as if he knew.

"No," she said.

"I don't believe you," he said, so calmly and serenely it would have made her think she was lying even if she wasn't.

"What, do I just reek of someone who needs someone to love?"

"Are you a virgin?"

"Isn't that an invasive question?"

"I'm your therapist. It's my job to be invasive."

She stared at him. Fine, she could be honest about this one. It would be interesting to see his reaction.

"No," she said coldly.

"Well?"

"I have had sex one time, with one man. I fucked him and I killed him as I did it. To survive."

He didn't falter. He just continued to look at her without talking. She knew this was so she would fill the silence, and she couldn't help but fall for the trick.

"I was captured by a community who said they would allow me to be safe. Like this one."

"Exactly like this one?"

"Well, no."

"How was it different?"

She hesitated. "They were using women to repopulate the earth. They gave us no choice and forced us to do as we were told."

"Why did you not refuse?"

"Because I wouldn't have escaped that way. The only way was to go along with it and then…"

She turned away.

"How did it make you feel?" he asked.

"What? Well, bad, it wasn't how they should treating–"

"I do not mean the morals of the community. I mean the man who you, as you so eloquently put it—*fucked and killed*." Hearing a swear word from his mouth was so unnatural. "How did you feel about that?"

"I don't know. I've never thought about it."

That wasn't a lie. She had never thought about it. At least, not consciously, anyway. She hadn't even told Dalton. It was just something she'd had to do.

Yet it had always been there, hiding behind her thoughts, the poisonous tale of her scorpion mind.

"Now you've thought about it, how does it make you feel?"

"That's such a cliché thing to ask. A therapist asking how it made me feel–"

"You're evading the question."

"I'm pointing out the odd situation. The world has ended and we are debating–"

"How. Did. It. Make. You. Feel."

She huffed.

"Fine. I—I felt nothing. Obviously, the immediate shock was bad, but then I had to escape, and I had to get Boy and this other girl and there was nothing I could do to dwell on it."

"Dwell on it now."

"No."

"Why not?"

"Because what good would that do?"

"Imagine some day you find a boy here—or a man, I should say—and you have sex with him. Do you really think you will do so without flashbacks or these panic attacks you keep getting? How would you have a healthy relationship?"

"I haven't really been thinking about a healthy relationship. I've been thinking about survival."

"Well, now's the time to shift your focus."

She scoffed.

"Why do you keep rejecting the idea that this could be a safe place for you to stay?"

"Because it's all so..."

"Perfect?"

She stood. She couldn't sit anymore so she stood, and she wandered, and went to the window where she saw children playing outside—*children,* and they were *playing,* and doing so *outside.*

She shook her head.

Fine, if he wanted honesty, he could have honesty.

"There was someone else," she admitted.

"Yes?"

"His name was Dalton."

"And?"

"And I thought I loved him."

"You thought you did?"

"Then I had to..."

"Yes?"

She shook her head.

"You had to what, Cia?"

She turned away.

"I think you need to say it. Aloud."

"Say what?"

"Say what you did."

"I..."

He looked at her expectantly.

"I killed him," she finally said. "He was a threat to me, and to Boy, so I did what I had to. I don't regret it."

"Don't you?"

Yes.

No.

I don't know!

She slumped back into her seat.

"There's someone here who seems to like me," she said, not sure why she was admitting it.

"Oh, yes?"

"His name is Hades."

"Oh, Hades. Yes, I know him. Good young man. Confident. I can see why you like him."

"I didn't say I like him."

He smiled.

"Stop doing that," she said.

"What?"

"That thing where you think you've read my mind."

"Okay. So, Hades. Why the hesitation?"

"I don't know. I don't even know if I could like someone. It's not something I've particularly thought about."

"Maybe now's the time to think about it."

"It's just..."

"You're worried?"

"Yes."

"About what?"

"About..."

"About Dalton."

It threw her off to hear his name said by someone else. His name had just been a thought, a thing she could erase from her mind every few hours. To hear someone else say his name meant he had existed. That what happened actually happened. It all seemed so far away...

"Well, Hades," Christoph said. "Why not spend some time with him?"

She shrugged.

"Because you still think you're living solely for survival?" he asked.

"That's what life is like now."

"Not in here, Cia. Not in here."

Could he be right?

Boy couldn't be happier.

He was learning about dinosaurs and learning about body language and having a life she never thought he could have.

Maybe she should think about more than survival.

Then again, that's how you get killed. You let your guard drop and you die. You should never stop concentrating on surviving.

"It's not my place to give advice," Christoph admitted. "It's my place to listen and ask the right questions. But in this situation, I think I will break the ethical code I live by and make such a suggestion."

Man, he used a lot of words.

"What?" she asked.

"Go for it," he said. "What do you have to lose?"

CHAPTER THIRTY-THREE

AGAINST HER BETTER JUDGEMENT, Cia briefly met with Hades and made plans to meet the following day.

It wasn't a date.

Except, it was.

But dates didn't exist anymore.

Except, they did.

Never did she imagine engaging in such menial tasks as dating... but she was. That was now her reality.

The reality where they were running from monsters and fighting and killing and doing unspeakable things to keep Boy safe was gone.

Yes, this place prompted many questions, many of which were yet to be answered. And she hadn't forgotten about Cathryn.

But Cathryn had made her choice.

She was too young to make it, but that was the world they lived in now.

Boy was happy. Graham was great. She was...

Content?

She'd sworn she wouldn't relax, wouldn't null her instinct

that had helped them survive this long. But maybe there was more to life. Maybe there was a purpose.

She said good night to Boy and watched him from his bedroom doorway, hovering, lingering her gaze upon him as he turned onto his side and instantly fell asleep, wrapped in a duvet. Comfortable. Snug. Warm.

She beamed with pride.

He was the reason she had kept going for so long, and he'd never know it.

Could he even understand it?

Sure, he could.

But could she explain it...

She was so proud of him. The way he had taken Graham's lessons with enthusiasm... it was remarkable.

And that was the one word she could consistently use to describe Boy: *remarkable*.

She backed away, closing the door, leaving him to sleep. Slowly, she crept along the hallway to her room next door. Even though it was a few steps, she didn't want the floorboards to creak. Just a few weeks ago she'd have wanted tiny noises to wake Boy up and alert him.

Not now.

Now, she wanted Boy to sleep in content silence, drifting off into a world where his unconscious took over and showed him all the delights it held.

She sauntered to her window. She was tired and wanted to get into bed, but first, she just wanted to relish it. Enjoy it.

The creatures didn't come close to the community, for whatever reason.

Yes, there were questions about why, but do you know what—they were safe! Whatever repellent the community had found was working. Ant spray kept ants away, maybe they had found something that fought off bigger creatures.

She hadn't seen a Thoral or a Maskete or a Lisker since that hunting incident, and even longer before that.

And, hey, she did not miss them.

It was a difficult adjustment, but now she was here she did not want to leave.

So she'd be their warrior.

She'd hunt with them, fight with them, and keep these people safe if that's what kept her and Boy safe. She would do all those things and more, if that's what this community required her to do.

She yawned. Rubbed her eyes.

Was this moment of reflection the effect her session with Christoph?

No, it was more than that.

It was a deeper change.

Something resembling happiness.

She closed the curtains.

She had one more thing to do before she slept.

She stood beside her bed. Lifted her pillow. Stared admiringly at the curved blade of the knife she kept ready, just in case.

She lifted that knife.

Twisted it. Marvelled at it.

Then dropped it by her side.

She walked over to the cupboard, opened the first drawer, and placed the knife inside, next to her socks.

With a final glance, like one you would give to a pet you were saying goodbye to, she took her eyes away and closed the drawer.

She would sleep without it.

It was there if she needed it, but for now, no one would attack her in her sleep.

She needn't keep in beneath her pillow.

And, what's more, as she lay her head down upon the pillow, she felt it sink further and provide more comfort than it previously had. It was as if the removal of the weapon had improved the bed's comfort.

The moonlight outside her window was shut out.

The streets were silent.

And her body was fatigued.

She closed her eyes and fell into a deep, wonderful sleep.

CHAPTER THIRTY-FOUR

A WALK along a stream and an ice cream on a bench. It was a surreal day, but a perfect one. Cia had forced herself to accept that it was happening, that she was on a date, with a handsome man, and that she was content to be so.

He seemed nice.

He probably wouldn't try to kill her.

She chuckled at the morbidity of the thought, then grew cold at her chuckles.

"You are really going for the ice cream," Hades observed, and Cia immediately felt subconscious.

Yes, she had been devouring that ice cream—but she hadn't had one since she was a child. She'd forgotten ice cream existed. She had forgotten the way it tasted. It was cold yet satisfying. Perfect texture against her tongue.

Damn, it was good.

"Sorry," she said. "I haven't had one of these in so long."

"Tell me about it," Hades said, licking his with far more constraint. "When I heard that someone here knew how to make ice cream, and was going to serve it from a van, I felt like I was eight again."

She knew what he meant. The taste made her feel like a child, taking her back to a place of pointless nostalgia where there were no creatures and her dad still loved her enough to protect her.

They finished their ice creams, and she munched down the rest of the cone and promptly wanted another one. She then realised how much silence she had left and looked uncomfortably to Hades.

Something glistened briefly in the sunlight. Something around his neck.

"It's a necklace," he said.

It was a thick chain with something at the end, like a little circle resting in the centre of his chest. He took it out and opened up this circle, revealing a picture of a woman with brown hair and kind eyes.

"It's my mum," Hades admitted.

"Where is she?" she asked, thinking this was better than asking *is she dead* and instantly regretting how reckless this question was.

"It's okay," he said, and she became very aware how easy her emotions were to read. "She died."

"Oh."

"It was a few weeks before the creatures rose, actually. Which makes me feel better in a way. That she died before having to witness what happened to the world."

It was a strange way of looking at things she hadn't thought of, but it made sense in a way. Perhaps they shouldn't feel sad for those who went before, and instead feel happy for what they didn't have to face.

"She gave this to me," Hades continued. "It's the only thing I have left of her."

Cia reached out to hold it, to see the picture more clearly. Hade's hand brushed against hers and she felt both excited and terrified at the same time. A wave of anxiety overcame her, the kind of nerves she felt before a panic attack, and she willed it away.

She rested her hand on her lap and he reached his hand across and rested his on hers too.

"I've had a really nice time with you," he said.

She smiled.

"Me too," she eventually replied.

His arm lifted from her hand and rested on the bench behind her. He leant closer, and she prepared for attack then quelled her instincts as he rested his forehead against hers.

He smiled as his lips came closer and they pressed against hers gently, so gently, ever so gently, and she let it and she hated it and loved it and he pressed harder and suddenly she was back outside, with Dalton, her lips against his, the first of their kisses where he meant it and the second of his kisses where he didn't because he had seen what she had done on the CCTV and was he already planning to kill her then was he already planning to hurt her it was a kiss he didn't mean and suddenly she was sticking a knife through his foot and she was watching him die and she was burying herself in the corner and crying as she listened to the Masketes tear him apart and—

She leapt to her feet and her feet gave way. She landed on her hands.

Hades rushed to her side and put his arms around her and he probably asked if she was okay but the words faded like she was underwater, they were there but not quite, and she felt vomit come to her mouth and she spat blood and bile onto the street.

"Let's get you to the doctor," he said, and she lifted her hand to brush him off.

She looked up at him and Dalton was standing there but it wasn't Dalton yet it was and–

She was crying.

She hadn't realised it, but she was.

She stood.

The thought faded and Hades looked at her with concern, everyone here was so damn concerned.

"Are you okay?" he asked.

"Yes, I, just... stay away from me."

She turned and marched away with her arms folded. She heard his footsteps go after her and stop.

She kept walking until she was back to Graham's porch where he sat with her and she buried her head as she cried.

Graham didn't leave, nor did he approach her.

Because he understood what it was like out there.

And he understood when to leave someone alone.

NOW

CHAPTER THIRTY-FIVE

She steps between bodies like avoiding cracks in the pavement.

This is what this life is now, isn't it?

An ocean of death?

She was foolish to think anything but it. To neglect her survivor's instinct. She had let herself be conned by comfort, duped by duplicity, masked my mistruths.

She looks for a face she knows. Some she recognises from passing in the street or wayward glances or from buying an ice cream.

But there aren't many faces left.

Yet, she does see someone she thinks she knows.

It looks like him, like the boy she thought she had a crush on.

Hades, his name was.

Of course, it isn't him.

She knows that.

It can't be. It's impossible.

She saw him die before any of this happened, so it can't be him.

But she pretends it is.

Convinces herself because she wants to see him again, just briefly.

And, as she convinces herself, this stranger becomes the man he isn't.

She looks at him and gasps, shocked that he is here, but not sad.

He knew, after all.

He knew all along.

Does that make him more or less deserving of death?

The answer is: *neither*.

No one is more or less deserving any more. People die and people live and sometimes it's more of one than the other, but that's how it is. People exist without living and live without dying and die without caring.

She doesn't feel guilt, because guilt no longer serves a function. Guilt was for a time when remorse appeased people around you.

There are no people around here.

Only dead ones, and they don't deserve an opinion.

Still, she walks up to this man she has assigned to the corpse and stops.

She crouches.

Looks over his stunned face.

There is a slight slash down his cheek, and a large slash down his open chest.

His eyes are open.

As are his lips.

Those lips that touched hers. Briefly. Before she had an attack of anxiety that she thought was hindering her comfort but was in fact warning her of dangers to come.

"I'm sorry," she says, because that's what she's supposed to say, isn't it?

It's only for the deceased onlookers.

It's only for show.

She doesn't feel sorry. She feels nothing anymore.

She just feels...

Empty yet full.

Light yet heavy.

Angrily content with being painfully numb.

She places her hand on his lips. Those lips that prompted so much hysteria and stress and oh how she realises how little it mattered now.

But it isn't really him.

Hades is dead like the others. Like all of them.

He died before this happened.

She saw it.

And this stranger...

Who killed him?

Did she?

Did she kill any of them?

Well, that would be a matter of opinion. Subjectivity in its finest glory.

She leans down and placed her lips against this stranger's.

She has no flashback now. No return to a life she will now resume, no glance at a life that once was and now is.

Dalton is no longer in her mind.

He is lower down on her list of murders now.

If you call this murder, that is.

You could call it justice. But, then again, you'd be missing the point, wouldn't you?

She lifts her lips, finding no moisture or warmth. If only she'd kissed him like this a few days ago, she may have experienced a brief, joyous flutter she could now reminisce about.

She does not regret, but she wonders *what if?*

What if she'd been able to kiss him?
If he had been a part of her life?
If it mattered?
She stands.
"Goodbye, Hades," she says.
And she moves on.

THEN

CHAPTER THIRTY-SIX

CIA SPENT another evening sat on the porch, frantically still, as Graham taught Boy how to conform to this new society he had never truly experienced.

She watched him learning about body language and subtext and what people say and do and how to interpret it, and she tuned out the voices, and just watched in content silence.

Boy was smiling.

Not just smiling like when he had some grapes for lunch, or when they didn't have to run from a monster, or when he slept somewhere more comfortable than mud under a log.

No, he was *really* smiling.

Like he was taking great pleasure in achieving something, like his confidence was growing, like he was able to flourish.

Such a life he could now have.

A life she had finally accepted, finally come to terms with living. This was good. It was great. It was perfect.

Too perfect, but she had pushed that thought away.

It was real.

She hadn't believed it, but she did now.

It is real.

And she felt a pang of guilt for how she had treated Hades.

He'd kissed her. She freaked out; to him, inexplicably so. She had just collapsed and said goodbye. Maybe she owed him an explanation.

No, she didn't owe anyone anything.

But maybe it would be good for her to just talk to Dalton.

No, not Dalton—Hades.

Dammit.

That was the problem, the only qualm with this place—that her instincts, acquired from so much fighting, had prevented her from adjusting.

When she was young, her dad had a friend that came to her eighth birthday party. A balloon popped, and he started freaking out and her dad had to take him outside.

Her dad had, later that night, explained that he had been in a place called Afghanistan. That he had returned from a war, and a balloon bursting reminded him of that war.

Through her child's eyes, she hadn't understood. She had just seen him as the idiot who almost wrecked her party. She wanted to help him, but he had distracted everyone from the forthcoming cake.

Now, she understood.

He had been in a war zone, and he couldn't adjust.

You adapt to that war zone, then when you come out of it, your environment changes but you don't.

But Dalton couldn't understand that.

So maybe she should–

Shit!

Hades, not Dalton!

She did it again.

And, just as she cursed herself for doing it, she was back kissing Hades, and then she was back kissing Dalton. That cold kiss he did not reciprocate. That kiss of death, the one before he lost it, the one after he knew what she had done to his friends, to the sanctity.

Her arms shook. Her legs buckled. Her heart thudded.

No, not again.

She felt her breath catch; she began wheezing, and then–

No.

Not this time.

She closed her eyes.

Told herself that Dalton was gone.

Dead.

Fed to the Masketes.

He was not coming back. He was not hurting her, or Boy.

And Dalton was not Hades.

She controlled her breathing. Concentrated on in, out, in, out. Listened to her breath, watching her own chest rise.

Dalton was gone.

She said it to herself again.

Dalton is gone. Dalton is gone. Dalton is gone.

And, just like that, the panic attack was over before it had begun.

She was back on the porch, watching Boy learn contentedly.

Neither Boy nor Graham had noticed.

Which was good. It meant the panic attack hadn't been that bad.

And she had brought herself back. From the strength this place had given her, she had readjusted her mind set.

Maybe if she could readjust that little bit, she could readjust to it all.

Permanently.

Maybe, just maybe, this was the life she was meant to live.

CHAPTER THIRTY-SEVEN

CIA AND BOY took to their afternoon stroll with a mild delight. The sun was high in the sky, people were happily doing their jobs, and they were walking peacefully without danger ready to pounce at any moment.

Some people even said hello. She must look different, she thought; happier, for people to break from their chores to smile at her, to wish her a good afternoon, to enquire how she was.

Eventually, they reached Hades' house.

She paused. Looked at it. Considered what she would say, and she panicked, thinking she should have thought more carefully about this, should have contemplated in more detail what she was going to–

No.

She had to stop it.

This was stage fright. Nerves. Pre-talk jitters.

She would just explain what happened, why it happened, and let him know it wasn't because of him.

"Can you wait here?" she said to Boy. "I just need to speak to someone."

He nodded. Even Boy was content to be left alone for a period of time. Something she had never imagined.

He found a bench where he sat and ended up in conversation with someone working on a vegetable patch.

Cia approached the door, went to knock, hesitated, then noticed the door was already open. She pushed it and it creaked open further.

"Hello?" she shouted.

No answer.

She stepped in.

"Hello? Hades, are you there?"

Nothing.

But she heard shuffling. There was definitely something.

Powered by instinct, she strode into the house and into the dining room, where she found... Ryker.

"What are you doing here?" Cia asked, regretting how irately she had asked it.

"Nice to see you, too," Ryker said.

"Where is Hades?"

Ryker had looked to be going through some drawers. Why was he going through drawers?

"He's gone," Ryker said.

"Gone?"

"Yes. On a mission. He hasn't returned." Ryker paused, looked at her, then added, "Yet."

"But... where has he gone?"

Ryker looked her up and down.

"On a mission."

He closed the drawers and walked up to her.

"What were you looking for?" Cia asked.

"Is there a reason you are here?"

Cia paused. Perhaps it was as much of a surprise for Ryker as it was for her to see him.

"I was looking for Hades. I—I wanted to talk to him."

"Like I said, he's on a mission."

Ryker looked to her expectantly, as if she was meant to do something. Cia was about to ask what, then she realised he was waiting for her to leave.

"When will he be back?" she asked.

"I don't know, Cia, but I have things to do here."

"Here? In Hades' home?"

"Yes."

"Did Hades ask you to do it?"

Ryker frowned. "Is it any of your business?"

No.

It probably wasn't.

If anything, she was likely to be the person intruding.

She nodded, backed away, and paused by the stairs, looking up and listening.

He didn't seem to be here.

Maybe she'd try again after their hunt that afternoon. Or tomorrow. Or whenever he was back.

She left the house to see Boy playing with a puppy. She smiled at the delight on Boy's face and promptly forgot about the perturbing conversation she had just had.

CHAPTER THIRTY-EIGHT

RYKER WATCHED Cia leave with Boy, off to enjoy the luxuries of civilisation.

He'd never met a girl like her before.

She was tenacious, inquisitive, and stubborn.

Both good and bad assets to have.

She was a wonderful contributor here; a fierce warrior who would defend this community with all she had.

But she was also a burden.

Someone who would never just accept things as they were.

And if she wouldn't accept Hades' disappearance, how was she going to accept his partaking in the event?

Hades had agreed to his invitation.

Eventually.

After a fight outside the walls that Ryker inevitably won.

In the end, Hades knew it was a responsibility that someone would have to take on at some point. There was no way around it; the event had to happen, and he had to be involved.

But Cia would not see it that way.

Ryker was sure of that.

She would not agree to live in a community where such things happened.

The community saw it as a necessity. They saw it as an unwanted importance, a regretful expense.

She would see it as an atrocity.

And he liked her, truly, he did.

And it was a shame.

Because the more and more she did not accept...

The more and more she asked questions...

The more and more she would not adjust to Boy's future involvement in the event...

The more Ryker realised he would have to kill her.

CHAPTER THIRTY-NINE

AGAINST HER BETTER JUDGEMENT, Cia spent most of her expedition that afternoon ruminating about the sudden disappearance of Hades.

It was not unfeasible, nor was it unprecedented, for Hades to be sent on a mission. That was his role within this society—to stray beyond the walls and investigate or learn or do whatever it is they do when they roam the real world. He had no obligation to tell her when he was leaving, nor did he have reason to, especially after how their date ended.

It just felt like Ryker was being dishonest.

She knew it was just familiar feelings resurfacing. She had come to terms with this community and her presence in it. She was content to be here, happy even.

It just felt the same way it did when Cathryn supposedly ran away.

Suspicious. Unsettling. Unnerving.

But those were just old feelings resurfacing. It was the caution that constant survival had embedded into her, that was all.

She had to tell herself to stop thinking about it.

Ryker led the group, followed by the same three burly men who had been on the last expedition. It was part hunt, part checking that there were no more Wasters. She was not there for the hunting part; she was there to protect the group, which felt strange considering they were all large men.

But, as Ryker pointed out, she had the experience. She knew what it was like out there. She knew how to hear a Waster coming.

Strange, that—how he only referenced the dangers posed to them by Wasters, and not any of the other creatures.

Ryker lifted his fist, and the group halted. He had seen something, and was aiming his rifle, as were the rest of the group.

Cia looked around.

She did not have a rifle. She had a knife. She knew little about operating guns, and besides, she found a gun difficult to aim.

A knife was easy to aim—you just swung it toward the throat.

She looked behind herself, to the side, peering all around. The others were focussed on the animal—a deer, she had heard Ryker mention—and it was her job to focus on threats, to ensure they were safe as they hunted this deer.

Something in the distance caught her attention. Something glistening, poking out from a group of leaves.

Something that intrigued her, though she wasn't sure why.

She meandered away from the group. They barely noticed, concentrating on the deer and readying their guns to fire. She moved in the opposite direction, toward this glistening item.

She crouched beside it. Stroked a few wayward leaves out of the way.

It was a necklace.

The chain was chunky, and on the end was a pendant.

She opened the pendant.

A woman with brown hair looked up at her.

The picture seemed familiar.

In fact, the whole necklace seemed familiar.

And, just as she recognised the familiarity, a sudden surge of memory imploded into her thoughts.

A memory of a day ago, as she sat beside Hades, and he showed her his necklace, told her the story of his mum, how she died, and...

Oh, God...

She lifted the necklace from the leaves. Looked back at the rest of the group.

None of them had seen her.

Could she be mistaken?

There were many necklaces, many with thick chains; people were bound to wear them. It could be anyone's.

But she knew it was denial.

Anybody could carry a chain, but not just anyone could carry a chain with a picture of Hades' mother.

The group fired their guns. A cheer of rejoice followed as they celebrated their kill. They began fast-paced talking of what to do with it, how to transport it home, how to share it out, what a good kill it was and so on and so forth.

None of them looked back at Cia.

Cia, staring at them with the necklace in hand.

Her first instinct was to confront Ryker. To march up to him, or to get him alone when they get back.

But to what avail?

What good would that be?

She had confronted him about many things and every time—every damn time—she received the same answers.

He always looked at her like she it was just because she

was struggling to adjust to a world where she didn't have to fight, where not everything was the horror she assumed it was.

So she pocketed it.

Saved it for later.

This community had become everything, and this could shatter that, and she didn't want it to.

Ryker had promised her answers, but they were not forthcoming.

Maybe she would have to acquire them in other ways.

CHAPTER FORTY

ONCE THEY RETURNED to the community, a dead stag resting over the shoulders of two men who gleefully carried it to the butchers, Ryker turned to Cia and thanked her for her work.

"I didn't really do much," admitted Cia.

"No, you did," said Ryker. "I saw you, looking around for us, checking we were safe. Just because you didn't fight anyone doesn't mean you did nothing. I just wanted you to know you're doing well."

Cia nodded nervously; she wasn't used to compliments, and she was wary what she may be about to discover.

She walked as if she was returning home, long enough for Ryker to take his eyes off her and direct himself toward Arnold's office. Ryker nodded at Arnold, who stood in his window, just as he entered the building. Cia waited a little more, then crouched and ran to the entrance Ryker had just disappeared through.

She saw Ryker and Arnold meet each other at the base of the stairs, so she waited outside the door and watched from her hidden position.

They talked with stern, serious faces, then nodded. They both walked into the building—but they did not return to Arnold's office. Instead, they began a confident, meaningful stride in the opposite direction.

Once they were out of sight, Cia opened the door just wide enough for her to sneak in. A glance back to check no one had seen her, and she was inside. She walked lightly to the edge of the corridor and peered around.

Arnold and Ryker disappeared around the other end of the corridor. She snuck out from her position and, keeping herself low, rushed to the end they had just disappeared behind.

Down the end of another long corridor, they walked out of a backdoor and into the outside. Cia followed, then paused by the door and watched through its small window.

Out the back of the building was a long garden path leading to a set of wooden stairs. The stairs themselves looked sturdy and new. They did not creak as Arnold and Ryker began to ascend them.

They must have built them after the creatures rose. It was a strange thing to build following the end of the world.

Cia left the building and followed them, keeping her distance, and moving from cover to cover. The steps kept rising and rising, so much so it was easy for her to linger behind and remain out of view.

After much climbing, the stairs took them to a small podium that hovered over the edge of the wall that surrounded the community.

Here, Arnold and Ryker paused, and they talked to someone who was already on the podium.

Cia couldn't quite make out who it was, but the conversation did not look like a light one. Their faces were empty, and the conversation was firm.

Cia attempted to move a little closer, just close enough that she could hide on a step low enough for them not to see her, but high enough that she could eavesdrop on what they were saying.

"Are you ready?" Ryker asked.

"Yes," came a man's voice.

"Are you willing?" Arnold asked.

The man's voice did not reply.

"I said, are you willing?"

"If you're asking whether I wish to do this, then no."

"It is an honour," interjected Ryker.

"It is a necessity," said the man.

Cia peered forward, reaching her stare further and further, until she could see more of this man. She saw a familiar hand that led to a strong arm that led to the distraught face of...

Hades.

His hands were bound in front of him, and his body was fixed to the podium.

"It's time," said Arnold.

Ryker tied a rope around the rope that bound Hades' fists.

To Cia's astonishment, Hades did not fight it. He was reluctant and despondent, but he allowed Ryker to attach this rope and hike his hands up, higher and higher, until Hades' hands were above his head and he was dangling with his toes just about scraping the ground.

Ryker took out a knife and, with no pause or hesitation, slit Hades' right wrist, then his left. Blood trickled out, a river down his arm.

Ryker stood to Hades' left, Arnold stood to Hades' right, and, in unison, they took to their knees and bowed their heads. Together, they remained in this position of worship.

Above them, a group of creatures circled in the sky. A squawk and a screech and they descended lower, lower, until they were hovering before the podium; a group of Masketes, hungry and ready.

The biggest of the Masketes floated forward, hovering, screeching its war-cry.

Ryker and Arnold did not run. In fact, they did not move. They remained focussed in their position, heads down, on one knee.

Hades cried.

That confident face, that warm swagger, it all fell from his body and he began to struggle. Whatever he had agreed to, he was now changing his mind, and tears were running down his cheeks.

"No, please," he began to murmur. "Please, I don't want to do this, I change my mind, it's not an honour, it's not a necessity, I want to live, please, please..."

Ryker and Arnold remained as they were.

The Maskete swooped at Hades and, with its mouth outstretched, sunk its jaw around his neck. It pulled and yanked, then finally took Hades' head clean off.

The Maskete threw the head behind itself, a look of wide-eyed terror still adorning its face, and allowed the other Masketes fight among themselves for it.

The Maskete then landed on the podium, inches from the still unmoved Ryker and Arnold, and devoured the rest of the body. It took seconds until all that was left of Hades was a blood-streaked podium, torn rags, and the occasional bone or liver or heart.

With Hades opened up, the Maskete lifted out his insides; his intestines and liver and heart; and threw them backwards, allowing the other Masketes to catch them and swallow them whole.

The Maskete sniffed Arnold and Ryker, then took off, launching into the sky, followed by the rest, until all of them had disappeared.

Cia couldn't move.

Her open mouth stuttered a few incomprehensible syllables.

But she had to move.

Because Ryker and Arnold were now standing, and she did not want to be noticed.

She retreated backwards down the stairs, until she was completely out of earshot, then turn and belted back through the building and into the streets.

CHAPTER FORTY-ONE

EVERY STEP CIA took was different.

The people going about their chores had grim expressions, the buildings were darker and more ominous, and the bare streets were paved with blood only she could see.

Despite the terror that raged her mind, she took each step slowly, stuck in a static catastrophe. Her body had stiffened. Her forehead was dripping with sweat. Her heart was thumping against the constraint of her ribs.

Denial was her first instinct.

Was there any way she could explain what she'd just witnessed?

Any way at all that she could have misinterpreted?

She scoffed the thought away and shook her head to herself. There was no way you can see murder as anything other than murder.

Then again, she'd killed. Dalton had seen her killing as unjust, but she hadn't.

Was there any way that...

No.

She was just trying to find something, desperate to find a way to un-taint the tainted walls of this community.

Was that how the creatures stayed away?

Because they gave them enough to feed?

Slowly and cautiously, she approached her home.

Home.

Could she still call it her home?

Isn't a home somewhere you meant to feel safe?

Boy sat on the porch with Graham. Once Graham saw her, he raised his hand and smiled. She tried raising a hand back, but it didn't lift very far.

As she approached, his delight at seeing her morphed to concern. From his expression, she realised that she must look dreadful.

"Is everything okay?" he asked.

Is everything okay?

What a question.

She looked to Boy, blissfully unaware, contentedly happy in this new place, where he could learn about body language and learn about dinosaurs and feel safe.

Safe.

What does that even mean?

"Cia?" Graham prompted, and she realised she had turned catatonic.

"Yeah?" she said, though she wasn't sure how much of the word came out.

"I said, are you okay? You look terrible."

She went to explain what she'd just seen, but then she thought—*does he know?*

She looked over her shoulder at a woman carrying a box of crops.

Does she know?

Do all those people working hard for their community, all

those people performing their roles, smiling at her as she walked past, being nice to Boy—do they know?

Or are they blissfully unaware?

"I'm..." Cia went to answer, but she lost the words.

"Cia, what is going on?" Graham asked, evidently concerned, and she knew she had to say something.

"Graham," she began, forcing her voice to come out, "how much do you know about this place?"

"What do you mean?"

"As in, do you know why the creatures stay away? Why they don't attack?"

Graham shrugged.

"I know what I need to know."

What did that even mean?

I know what I need to know.

Cia had no way of deciphering that.

Did that mean he just took it on faith, or did that mean he knew, to some extent, what Arnold and Ryker were doing?

Then a thought hit her so hard it took her off her feet and onto her knees.

Cathryn.

Did she really runaway?

Oh, God.

Did they feed her alive to the creatures? Did she have to suffer what Hades...

She covered her face. She did not want Graham or Boy to see her cry.

"Cia?" Graham said, and he came to her side, kneeling down, putting his hand on her back.

"Come on, how about you go lie down," he suggested.

Lie down?

"I'll take care of Boy."

"No!" she snapped.

She would not leave Boy. Not now, never.

"What is it?" Graham asked.

"Boy comes with me," Cia said.

"He's safe with me, trust me."

Cia looked up at him.

Was he safe with him?

Was anyone safe with anyone?

Was she next? Was that the real reason they had brought her in?

So many questions, so little answers, and so much anxiety that she struggled to keep her grip on the one thing that had previously willed away the fears—*this place.*

This had been her salvation, Boy's salvation, their way out of the miserable life of being walking food, surviving from one minute to the next.

She didn't want to let go of this new hope; she wanted to cling onto it, keep her grip.

But she had just watched them sacrifice a man she cared about.

She needed to think, and she needed to be alone.

With Boy.

She stood, grabbed Boy's arm, and pulled him with her.

"Rosy!" he objected, but she ignored it, and she dragged him away.

"Cia?" shouted Graham, but she ignored him.

Once she had entered her house, she locked the door.

But would that be enough?

It was their community; would they not have a key?

She bolted the door. Picked up a chair and propped it against the door handle, then did the same with the back door.

"Rosy, what's happening?" Boy asked, his voice so innocent, his question so unknowing.

"We're going to sleep like we used to tonight," she said. "Together. How would you like that?"

He seemed to think about that for a moment, then nodded eagerly.

Darkness was descending outside, but she did not plan on sleeping herself.

They lay on the sofa, Cia behind Boy with her arm around him, listening to the sound of him snoring like she had for so many nights, adamantly staying awake.

CHAPTER FORTY-TWO

Cia woke up in the darkest part of the night.

How had she fallen asleep?

She lay on her back on the sofa, Boy soundly asleep, his arm draped across her chest. His breath puffed against her chin and she never felt smaller.

A muffled bang sounded from outside the house.

Was that what had woken her up?

Another bang.

Was this it?

Were they outside her house?

Had they seen her? Were they coming for her?

She gently lifted Boy's arm from around her and shifted his much greater weight away. She stepped over his tall body and placed her feet gently on the carpet. Even though her feet wouldn't make a sound, she stepped lightly anyway, instinctively being cautious.

She paused and listened.

Another muffled bang, but it wasn't in the house, nor was it against the door or the wall.

She crept to the window, moved the curtain marginally apart, and peered out.

She could see little in the darkness. She squinted and peered and struggled to see where the noise was coming from, but then another muffled bang came, and her eyes quickly directed themselves next door.

Graham's house.

Three of them. Big, burly men. Knocking on his door. She didn't recognise any of them.

"Come on, Graham," one of them said. "You knew it was your turn."

Your turn?

She had no definite proof of what that meant, but she made a quick assumption and stubbornly stuck to it.

Looking back at Boy, she hesitated.

Could she leave him alone?

Next door, one of them barged open the door.

She couldn't let them get to Graham.

She grabbed the front door key, rushed to it, unbolted and removed the chair she'd propped against it, and flung herself out.

She took a moment to lock the door, then buried the key in her pocket.

There was no point being subtle, no point sneaking up on them—what help would that be?

"Oi!" she shouted.

Two of the men looked at her. Where was the third?

"What's going on?" she shouted.

"Go back inside," said one of the men. "This doesn't concern you."

"It does, what are you doing?"

"Go back to bed," said another assertively. "You don't know what you're messing with."

From the doorway came the third man, dragging out Graham, his arms interlocked between Graham's elbows.

"No!" Cia shouted, and rushed to this man, trying to pull him off Graham.

"Cia, stop," Graham said. "It's okay."

"No!" she repeated.

It was not okay.

Whether or not Graham knew what they were doing, it was not okay.

She needed Graham.

He was the only one who understood her, the only one she trusted with Boy.

They couldn't hurt him, they couldn't.

One of the other men pushed Cia away. She fell onto her back but quickly launched herself back up again. She punched the third guy's head, repeatedly; even though it had little effect, she did it, until one of the others pushed her away.

"Back off!" he demanded. "This does not concern you!"

"Get off him!" Cia said, ignoring the objections.

"Cia," Graham said, in as calm a voice as he had ever used. "Please. It's okay."

"No, it's not," she said, and continued battering at the man holding him captive.

"Will someone deal with this bitch?" said the third man.

One of the other men stepped forward, and she swung her fist so hard into his Adam's apple he fell to his knees and choked.

"Cia!" Graham shouted, but she ignored him.

She jumped onto the back of the man holding him captive and dug her teeth into the side of his neck. He tried to shake her off, but she dug in, and allowed herself to be swung about, clinging on and digging in further.

The man couldn't help but scream out, and she noticed a few twitches of curtains in the house across the street, but she didn't care. She continued to bite, to cling on, until she felt blood run through her mouth and trickle down her chin.

"Someone fucking get her off me!"

One of the other men tried to pull her off, pulled at her with all his masculine might, but it was no match for her determination.

She dug her canines in and relished the taste of red; it was what she was used to. These people were bigger and stronger, but they had not fought the fights Cia had.

Graham stood, looking at her somewhere between fright and astonishment. She willed him to run, but he didn't. He just remained, poised between telling her to stop and thanking her.

Then she saw one man lift a large plank of wood.

A thud against her skull and she saw nothing, feeling only the gravel against her head as she passed out.

CHAPTER FORTY-THREE

CIA WAS GROWING tired of awaking to an unfamiliar circumstance.

She tried to regather her thoughts, to fight the drowsiness, the grogginess. She was in her house, in her bed, she knew that. She could see Boy, his blurry figure, organising his toy dinosaurs across the room.

"Hey," came a voice.

Any lethargy was replaced with alarm.

Ryker sat on a chair beside her bed.

She went to get up, to fight, feeling her lip curl into a snarl.

He raised his hand and said, as coolly as he ever had, "It's okay, I'm not here to hurt you."

He paused, poised between lying down and sitting up.

"How do I know that?"

"Because if I was going to hurt you, then I would have done it when you were asleep."

She lay back down, cautiously, her head feeling heavy. She still kept her eyes on him, her body twitching in readiness to fight at any moment.

"I take it you need some answers," he said.

"Yeah. Yeah, I think so."

"What happened to Graham last night, he... well..."

Ryker seemed to be struggling, so Cia completed the sentence for him.

"Was being sacrificed to the creatures?"

Ryker looked confused.

"Just like you did to Hades, too, right? Yet, you said he was going on a mission."

Ryker smiled. "In a way, he was."

Cia frowned.

"In a way?"

"This isn't a perfect design, Cia, but it's one that keeps us living."

"A perfect design?"

"We were going to tell you all this. Eventually. We could hardly just explain that we sacrifice people as soon you enter, could we?"

"Why not?"

"Because then you would leave. You wouldn't settle in. You're far more likely to stay once you've decided this is your home."

"So you're conning me then?"

"No."

"And how long until it's me you sacrifice? Huh?"

Ryker hesitated. He shifted position and seemed to choose his words carefully.

"All throughout history," he said, "people have sacrificed what's precious to them to their gods. Their best lamb, their daughter, what have you—it has been something necessary to keep peace."

"You think these creatures are your gods?"

"You don't?"

"They are predators. Animals. They aren't divine or immortal."

"And they came straight from Hell, Cia. We are positive of that. They may not be the gods we want, but we've got them, and we need to appease them."

Cia's jaw hung open. Was she actually hearing this?

"And, to answer your earlier questions, how long until we choose you—we rarely, if ever, choose someone who is unwilling."

"Rarely?"

"Normally it's someone who has consented."

"Normally?"

He took a moment.

"The more precious the sacrifice, the longer they stay away. If we offer them someone older—"

"Like Graham," she interrupted.

"Fine. Like Graham. If we offer them someone like Graham, then we have days. Someone younger and we have weeks. Someone loved and useful and precious, well, that could give us far longer."

"So you're bargaining with other people's lives?"

"It isn't perfect, Cia, far from it. We know that. But this is how we survive, how we keep our community safe."

"Is that why the Wasters still attack you? Because they are the ones that serve the creatures, and they are envious that you are serving them instead?"

"We believe so, yes."

She rested her head back. This was a lot to take in, and she had a migraine coming.

She leant her head to the side and looked at Boy organising his dinosaurs, so blissfully unaware, just as she had been less than a day ago.

"So what, you don't have to sacrifice anyone else for a few days now?"

"Well, no. We tend to do all of our sacrifices in one go. So we may sacrifice someone else, and someone else, and the time we have accumulated to be left in peace adds up. Every few months, well... We have to do this again."

"Why not sacrifice Arnold? Surely killing your leader would give you far more time?"

"We need a leader, Cia. And, besides, we wouldn't be here if it weren't for Arnold."

"That's bullshit."

"That's the harsh truth. Hades knew it. And Graham knew it."

Boy paused, looked back at her, smiled, then returned to his activity.

"We really want you to stay, Cia. You're a great asset to us. We really hope you will adjust and—"

"How could I stay, knowing I'd be looking over my shoulder the whole time, wondering if I was next?"

Ryker looked down, taking a big, deep breath, and shrugged his shoulders.

"No reassurance I can give you will ever make you feel secure. You've just got to believe what's worth sacrificing to protect this community."

She scoffed and shook her head.

"Or would you rather be out there?" he asked, pointing to the walls outside the window. "Would you rather face potential death every minute of every day?"

"We survived pretty well out there, thank you."

"Yeah, and how much longer would you last? And what would be the point, Cia? In here, you stand a chance at a real life. So does Boy."

"We'll take our chances."

"Seriously, Cia, I urge you to reconsider–"

"I said, we'll take our chances," she repeated.

Ryker stopped arguing. Her resolve was strong, and she would not be dissuaded, and she could see that he knew that.

"We will gather our things and leave in a few hours."

Ryker reluctantly nodded.

"I really think you're making a big mistake," he said.

"You can go now."

She looked at him with those cold, cold eyes. She was angry, not just at him, but at how she was going to lose the life that was just too good to be true.

How could she be so stupid to think they could have something resembling a normal life, that society could exist as it once did?

Society had ended.

The world had ended.

This was what it was now.

Ryker stood. Looked to Boy. Looked to Cia.

"I said, you can go."

He did as he was told, turning and walking out of the room.

Cia put her pillow over her head so Boy couldn't hear her crying.

NOW

CHAPTER FORTY-FOUR

CIA ISN'T EVEN sure she feels anything anymore.

So much death rests on her hands, and she feels none of its weight.

All these bodies are indirectly because of her.

She feels love for Boy.

But all those other emotions she expects to suffer as she endures the human condition... guilt... solace... despair... she feels none of them.

She is comfortably empty.

It is time to leave. She has looked around long enough.

But she can't.

Despite the void she feels, there is something in her that makes her want to punish herself, makes her want the streets of murder to make her feel guilty.

She wants to force herself to look at it, so she will feel bad.

She seeks a face that would make her feel such a way, a familiar face, someone she felt some kind of attachment to.

And she finds it.

In the living room of the house that was once her home.

Christoph.

His old eyes looking tired and vacant, and his worn-out jacket looking livelier than him.

Christoph, the man who had helped her.

The man she had trusted.

The man who had betrayed her first.

She wishes he hadn't. Oh, how she wishes he hadn't.

He was the one person she wishes didn't have to pay for the sins of the society he was so embedded in.

But he knew, just as they did.

And he had his part in it.

And this is a death that she could not blame on any other creature—she could only blame it on herself.

She had confided and opened up and grown because of their conversations.

Now, there he is.

Laying there with his eyes up.

Her first kill in the community.

Her hands took this life.

This life was her responsibility.

It had been the onset of her rage.

And it had only been the beginning.

THEN

CHAPTER FORTY-FIVE

BOY SAT on the floor of the living room. Reading words he had only just learnt from a man who could no longer teach them.

She allowed him to continue reading, hesitating to leave. It was a hesitation that gave him his final few moments of community, of a feeling of safety. He loved it here and it would be tough for him to understand.

But hopefully, he would.

Someday.

She packed the final set of clothes into her bag and zipped it up. Then she placed the knife she had removed from beneath her pillow, so full of optimism, at the front. The bag was tough to zip, and she wasn't sure how much she should condemn herself to carry it, but she wanted to keep some luxuries.

She'd come to like them.

A gentle tap on the front door caught her attention.

She didn't answer it, but that didn't matter.

A few seconds went by and the door creaked open, just slightly, just enough for Christoph to push his head in.

"Cia?" he said, his voice kind, calm, so in contrast to the community's beliefs.

"I'm in here," she said, deciding she had nothing to lose by letting him say goodbye.

He closed the door behind him and shuffled in.

"I was wondering if maybe we could talk," he requested.

"Okay."

"Maybe... away from ears that might overhear."

She glanced at Boy.

They could go into the kitchen. He'd be okay. It was only in the next room. She'd hear if anything was wrong.

"Fine."

She walked through to the kitchen, leant on the side and folded her arms. Christoph stood in front of her, his hands clasping one another. He seemed to struggle for words, which felt odd for a psychiatrist, a supposed expert in human behaviour.

"I take it you know," Cia said, tired of waiting for him to start the conversation.

"Do you mind if I have a glass of water?" he asked and, without waiting for confirmation, took a glass and gulped down the entire thing in one.

He was sweating. And, as he turned back to Cia, she noticed he was fidgeting.

Cia went to ask what the matter was, but she had to know if he knew.

"Do you know about the sacrifices?"

He looked at her, holding her gaze, a visage of worry.

"Yes," he finally answered. "Yes, I know. Most do."

"And you're okay with it?"

"I wouldn't necessarily say that."

"But you allow it to happen?"

"What would I do otherwise? Object?"

"Why not?"

"And if my objections were successful, which I sincerely believe they would not be, what then? The creatures would batter down the walls or leap over them and kill everyone in here. It's a minority for the majority, I'm afraid."

"The minority?" Sudden flashbacks of herself fired into the forefront of her mind; quite a few years younger, being denied entrance to the sanctity while her dad went in ahead of her, because of her mixed heritage, because she was a *minority*. "It's funny, isn't it? Whenever the many decide that they must sacrifice things, it's the minorities who are the ones to fulfil the obligation."

"You're a smart girl, Cia. No—a smart *woman*. Your intellect will be wasted out there."

"I'll take my chances."

"It's a shame, though. Could I have another glass of water?"

He filled up another glass and drained it. His fidgeting was becoming more erratic. He was now shifting his weight from one foot to the other, looking around with beady glances.

"What's the matter?" Cia asked. Surely he couldn't be that upset at her leaving?

"I really do wish you would reconsider."

"It's not right, Christoph."

"But I really..." His voice drifted off, and he wiped his forehead on the back of his sleeve.

This was strange.

Odd.

Perturbing, even.

He was far too nervous. Why was he so nervous? It was as if he...

Cia froze.

Boy.

She went to leave the kitchen, but he sidestepped into her way.

"What are you doing?" she growled.

"I'm so, so, sorry Cia. They made me do this."

"Do what?"

"I really did not want to betray you. I–"

She barged Christoph out of the way and returned to the living room.

An empty living room.

"Boy?" she shouted.

No answer.

She looked behind the sofa, behind the chairs, obvious hiding places.

She rushed to the hallway, to the bathroom, to every room in the house, upstairs and downstairs.

She opened the front door and looked around.

"*Boy!*" she screamed.

Christoph appeared behind her.

"It's no use," he said. "The decision has been made. You may as well accept it."

She turned and looked at his face, his stupid face, his incredulous, twisting, twitching face, and rage coursed through her, that same rage that took her in the sanctity, with Dalton, and it was happening again, all over again, and Cia did not regret this feeling, she did not regret what she was about to do; it was all too much; she was going to explode going to burst going to, going to, going to...

She tried to breathe, but her lungs couldn't keep up.

She grabbed Christoph by the throat and, despite his far greater stature, marched him into the house, into the living room, and shoved him against the wall.

She opened her bag.

Withdrew the knife.

"Cia, please, I–"

"Where is he?"

"I—I don't–"

She dragged the knife down his chest.

He did nothing to stop her; he wasn't a fighter.

"Where is he?"

"I don't–"

She slid the knife into his gut, then quickly back out again.

"Where is he?"

"I don't–"

She swung the knife at his face and dug it into his cheek

Christoph took to his knees. He didn't run or fight.

Cia had been correct.

The people in here did not know how to survive.

"Tell me where they have taken him."

"I—I don't know, really I don't..."

Then you have no use.

She swung the knife and buried it into the side of his neck until all that remained visible was the handle. She took the knife back out again and the walls, the fireplace, the furniture, her face, her clothes, everything was painted with the blood of the betrayer.

She stuck his knife back into his throat a few more times and allowed his suffocating body to drop to the floor.

She didn't wait to see his death finish.

She left the house, ready to kill anyone else who stood in her way.

CHAPTER FORTY-SIX

CIA BURST out of the house, an animal unleashed, scouring the surroundings with her dilated pupils, her fists curling, her body shaking, ready to do whatever she had to, once again.

Once again.

Always the same story.

People underestimate her caring for Boy, undervalue it, think they could take him away and get away with it.

She would willingly kill everyone here to get to him if she had to.

A big, burly man walked up to her, putting his hand up.

"Cia," he said, but she heard none of it.

He had a gun, but she didn't care.

He approached, full of confidence that he could handle her.

But a gun and a set of muscles are nothing against a woman scorned.

"I'm afraid I've had instructions to keep you in your–"

She leapt upon him, landing on his chest and grabbing the back of his neck, digging her teeth into his gullet. He screamed out, tried to shove her off, but lost his ability to do so once she had scraped her knife down his spine. He collapsed to the floor, squirming and writhing as she stabbed him repeatedly in the back, over and over and over and over until she had just about begun to give him the punishment she deserved.

His body throbbed.

She knelt upon it and looked up at the voyeuristic eyes upon her.

People doing chores, carrying vegetables, carrying meat, greeting friends and stroking puppies and going for a leisurely walk, *all of them*, every single one, stopped—all of them watching.

Terrified.

They had seen nothing like this before; they were not prepared for what this world produced, for what *they* had produced, and Cia didn't care.

No—in fact, she loved it.

She relished it.

She was small. She was young. She was an image of innocence.

But they all underestimated the monster this world could create.

She launched herself forward with both arms and both legs and charged and they scattered, screaming and fleeing.

So many of them, so many that could take her if they all teamed up together, but they didn't.

Why?

Because they weren't like Cia.

She paused, looked around for what next.

Glanced over her shoulder at the body she had just created.

Saw a mother holding a baby glance at her, see the body, and run.

She didn't care.

In fact, she was a little proud for what she did to anyone prepared to hurt boy.

"*Boy!*" she screamed and awaited an answer.

There was no answer forthcoming.

"*Boy, where are you!*"

Nothing.

One of the hunters she had been with the other day stepped out of his building to see what the commotion was. She ran up to him quicker than he could comprehend and shoved the knife in his belly.

"Where is he?"

"What?"

He was so taken aback, so thrown off, so unaware of how to react, that he did nothing but accept the pain.

"*Where is Boy?*"

"I have no idea–"

She stuck her knife into his chest, nestling it beneath his ribs and upwards and he wheezed, coughed up blood like an overflowing milkshake, staring at her.

She would kill everyone here if she had to.

But she had to think.

Had to use her rage, but still have a clear plan.

And, just as she willed herself to regain some clarity, just as she let the hunter slide off the knife and wheeze upon the floor, she decided she knew where to go next.

She peered over her shoulder at Arnold's office.

There he was, standing in the window.

He did not look afraid.

He just stood there, like he had when she arrived.

Arms behind his back. Not reacting to the death of two of his men.

He retreated into his office.

With a scream she ran, belted forward, searing through the street, leaping over benches, stomping over crops, ignoring those that fled out of her way, ignoring the shouts of shock over the two bodies she left behind.

She barged into the doorway of the town hall and began the route down the corridor and up the stairs.

CHAPTER FORTY-SEVEN

THE DOOR WAS ALREADY OPEN.

Like he was waiting for her.

Like he expected it.

Like he saw her from above, watched her enter the building, and decided that he wouldn't need any protection.

Cia didn't know whether to be pleased or cautious or humiliated by the idea that he saw her as such a little threat.

Did he know what she could do?

What she had done?

She was prepared to slaughter anyone in her way, and just because he was the leader, the politician who had unlimited funds, it did not mean that he was exempt.

If anything, he deserved it most.

"Where is he?" Cia growled, standing in the doorway. She did not retreat, nor did she enter, not yet.

Arnold turned from the window, slipped his hands casually into his pockets, and smiled as if she was a niece or nephew come to show him the picture they'd drawn.

"Cia," Arnold said. "I was waiting for this day."

"What do you mean," she snarled, "you were waiting for this day?"

He smiled again, that patronising smile, and he mosied over to his desk where he poured whiskey from a decanter into a crystallised tumbler glass.

"I've already killed three of you," Cia told him, not quite believing that he understood the severity of the situation. "I am ready to kill you too."

"Oh, yes, I am quite aware of that."

"You should be scared."

"Yes, but, alas, I am not. And don't think that's because of your tiny stature. In fact, quite the contrary—I can see you are nimble and that the knife you hold in your hand, with blood of my people on it, is quite lethal. But you will not kill me."

Her blood coursed rage through her body. How wrong he was.

"I will," she said

"Oh, no, you won't. Because otherwise how will I tell you where Boy is being taken?"

She went to reply but didn't.

Suddenly, she thought, in a moment of clarity—could they be taking Boy to the podium where they killed Hades?

Then again, there could be more than one podium. Or there could be other stations they sacrifice him at. Or they may not even need a podium—maybe they are to tie him up outside and leave him there.

She couldn't be sure. She had to find out where he was; she didn't have time to search everywhere.

She saw some rope in the corner of the office.

Maybe that was the rope they used, and he was already dead.

"He's alive," Arnold said, as if he could see Cia's thoughts projecting into a bubble above her head. "Now sit."

He sat in his leather chair and sipped his whiskey, indicating the chair opposite.

Cia had no intention of sitting.

"Where is he?" she said.

"I said to sit."

"You're not the only one who'll know. I bet Ryker will too."

"Sit, please. Let me explain why we have taken him."

"I am *not* sitting."

Arnold held her gaze for a moment, and Cia felt herself unintentionally sneering.

"Fine," said Arnold, standing up and moving to the window. "As you wish."

"Where is he?"

"Cia, let me be honest with you, if you will. Is that okay? If I'm honest with you?"

She flexed her fingers around her knife.

She took a stride toward him.

There was only so much patience she could manage.

"You are a wonderful warrior," Arnold said. "An excellent survivalist. Someone who knows what to do in a grave situation. You are a great asset to our society, and we greatly need you."

"Where is–"

"But Boy isn't. Ryker wasn't even supposed to bring him here; he was only supposed to bring you—but there you were sauntering in on your first day with him at your side. It was there and then we knew he wouldn't last. He wouldn't have a place here."

"Where is he?"

"Come to your senses, Cia! Think about it—he holds you back! He has held you back out there I'm sure, and he has no purpose here. There is no job, no role, nothing he can do. He is just mentally off."

"He's autistic."

"He's retarded."

That was all he needed to say.

Cia charged forward, lifting the knife for his throat. He ducked to move out of the way, but Cia had expected that, and quickly lowered her knife instead.

She looked deep, deep into his eyes as she slid the knife into him. This time it was easier, like pushing through butter, though it became tougher the more she pushed.

"Tell me where he is," she said, but it was no good.

He couldn't talk. His mouth was muffled by the red gunk dribbling down his chin.

She swiped the knife out of him and he stayed on his knees, coughing, struggling, dying.

She was covered in the blood of others now. Her feet, her trousers, her vest. Everything.

Good.

It was her war paint.

No one would approach her without certainty of their fate.

But it was still not enough.

Cia wished to make a statement, and Arnold was not dying quickly enough.

She fetched the rope from the corner of the office.

She swung it around his neck. He tried to bat it away with a weak hand but he hadn't the energy. He was struggling and coughing and writhing and Cia was gaining a substantial amount of satisfaction from it.

She tied the rope as tightly as she could.

She fetched a chair and stood on it, tying the rope around

the top of the curtain rail above the grand window he used for his voyeuristic stares at the ants below.

She used the chair to smash the window. It took a few attempts, but eventually it shattered.

Arnold looked up at her.

She was sure she made out the word *please.*

She kicked him and he fell out of the window. His neck snapped, and he dangled there.

Everyone in the street stopped.

Some screamed.

Some came from far away to see what was happening.

They were all forced to watch as he hung until death, stuttering and grasping and reaching his arms out helplessly.

She stood in the window behind him so they all knew who had done it.

So they all could fear her.

And, amongst the crowd, she saw him.

Ryker.

He met her stare and ran.

But he ran into the village hall.

She knew he wasn't coming to find her.

He's going to the podium.

He was trying to ensure she didn't get to Boy.

She wasted no more time.

She turned and ran, retracing the steps she had snuck along to find Hades being murdered, hoping that Arnold was not lying, and that she was not too late.

CHAPTER FORTY-EIGHT

"*Boy!*"

No point being subtle now.

No point in anything but being loud and making her presence known.

If he was on the podium, she wanted him to know she was coming for him.

That he wasn't alone.

That he needn't be afraid.

She could see him already and it broke her heart. Not physically, of course, the stairs were steep and long, but she could fabricate an image of his face in her mind. Against her will, she saw his tears, his breakdown, his mortification—she saw him reciting their poem to himself, as if that would make a difference, until he'd recited it and recited it and she was still not there.

He would be bound, awaiting the inevitable.

He must be so scared.

It must hurt so much.

She stopped trying to resist the thought and used it

instead, used it to fight the aching, to fight the fatigue the steep ascent caused.

She could see the back of Ryker's legs. He was faster than her, and he was getting to Boy quicker, and she had to speed up, had to use the adrenaline, use the rage.

As she grew closer, she could hear Boy's tears, his screams, his pleas.

"Rosy! Rosy, please, where are you! *Rosy!*"

It shattered her. Broke her. Destroyed her.

She didn't want to see any pain in him; she hated it—but this was beyond pain. He wouldn't be able to understand. He'd thought he was safe here, that people were nice, that they let him stroke their puppies and let him say hello and taught him about body language and this—*this* he would not comprehend.

As she neared the top steps, the sight of Ryker halted her.

He stood there, blocking her way.

Boy's head turned, and he had to strain, but their eyes just about met. Circles and circles of rope bound him, so much he couldn't move, couldn't even shift his hand.

"*Rosy!*" he screamed.

"Boy..." she whimpered, and she cried, and he hated herself for it.

Why did this have to be how things were?

It was history repeating itself.

It was the same problem she'd had.

Separated by Masketes.

Separated by Dalton.

And now, separated by Ryker.

The man who had introduced her to a community where she could flourish, serve a purpose, and make a life worth living.

She had already come to terms with that image fading, like a perfectly finished painting ready to hang on the wall only to rip it down and shred it, destroying any resemblance of what the image once was.

Cia stopped.

She paused, a few steps down from him.

She had to think. Use her rage but use her mind as well.

Ryker wasn't like Arnold.

He had been outside the walls; he had fought; he had seen the world for what it was.

She had to be smart.

"There's no choice, Cia," Ryker said. "I know you won't take it, but I'm going to give you the opportunity to stop. To accept it. I know it's tough, but this is how we live now. This is how our community works. We have no choice but to–"

"Go to hell."

She took another step upwards.

Readied her knife.

Ryker sighed.

"I'm stronger than you, Cia," he said. "Remember our sparing in the gym? Remember how you lost? And that was me taking it easy on you."

Another step. She was three away.

"That was me on a good day," Cia said. "You've caught me on a bad one."

Ryker chuckled.

As if it was a joke.

As if it was all a joke.

Another stab of aggression and Cia had to quell it.

Two steps away.

"Please, Cia," he said. "See sense. If you want to be in our community–"

"I don't want to be in your community," she said. "And once I have Boy back, I will make sure no one will ever be in your community again."

It was Cia's turn to see anger meet Ryker's face.

"So you'll make all those innocent people pay because you don't like how things are done? They are people, Cia. Like you. *People.*"

One more step.

"People," she said, slowly and spitefully, "are the worst. They are less deserving of life than those creatures. And I intend to do away with all of them."

She was being extreme; she knew it, but she could see her words crawling beneath his skin, pushing at it, provoking his fury.

With a sudden breath, she swung the knife toward his throat.

He caught her wrist.

His grip was tight.

So tight, she felt her hand go numb.

And, as her hand grew more and more numb, her grip on the knife loosened, until, eventually, it fell out of her hand, and disappeared into the depths below.

She watched the knife fall into trees and shadows and her legs wobbled as she realised just how high up this podium was, and how precariously balanced she was on the steps.

She looked to Boy.

The growl of a Thoral shook the trees in the near distance.

Ryker looked to Boy, and she knew why.

Because that Thoral was coming for its sacrifice.

The ground began to shake, the feeling of a Thoral approaching from.

She tried to get past Ryker, but he shoved her out of the way.

The growl grew louder.

"I'm sorry you couldn't accept a better life," said Ryker.

Cia clenched her fists, readying them for war.

CHAPTER FORTY-NINE

The selfish, sordid, vile little bitch.

She claimed that the outside tainted her, that a life out there had made her find it difficult in here.

But she wasn't prepared for sacrifice.

How could someone claim to have survived out there, to have experienced such terrors, and not be prepared for sacrifice?

Her love was futile.

The child was in her way.

He wasn't just childish; he was... abnormal. Slow. Strange. Couldn't understand anything.

And his value to her made the value of his sacrifice all that much greater. Just think... months with no need to offer anyone else. The community would be so content to just go about their lives for months to come. It would be unprecedented; the longest they'd ever gone without having to give up one of their own.

And the Thoral was approaching.

He could hear it.

It wasn't long now.

"Move out my way," she said, as if she had power, as if her conviction gave her any authority.

Rage or no rage, experience or no experience, she was still a little girl. Puny in size and puny in nature. He could discard her of her knife with strength alone—imagine what greater advantage he had over still when he considered his cunning, reasonableness, superior skills.

She tried to push him and little happened.

He grabbed her wrists, and she went to headbutt him.

He leant his head back and her forehead just about brushed his chin.

She opened her mouth and aimed it at his throat. He swung his elbow into her jaw, and she collapsed.

That was a mistake, however, as she was now the other side of him.

She was now closest to Boy.

She leapt onto the podium, reaching out for him—but he jumped onto her calf and forced her onto her front.

He lifted her head and smacked it into the ground, leaving a few dots of blood, like someone had flicked a paintbrush over the podium.

Boy was crying.

Again, this forced her weakness to prevail. This gave it centre stage, gave him the superiority over her in yet another aspect of their fight.

The podium shook as the pounding of the Thoral grew stronger.

She pushed herself to her feet and faced him.

She lifted her arms to her face, in a fighting stance.

He chuckled.

"We already did this," he said. "Remember? You lost, pretty badly."

She ignored him and swung a fist which he ducked.

She swung another which he blocked and landed a heavy hand into her belly. She stumbled back, winded, and skidded to a stop at the edge of the podium.

A few stones tumbled backwards and collapsed into the abyss.

All he had to do was get her to over the edge.

Shame to waste her, as she could have been a great warrior, or an even better sacrifice, should she have continued to insist that she wouldn't be part of the community anymore.

He could give her one thing though—she was resilient.

She shook the pain away and breathed and went for him once more.

He blocked a fist, blocked a fist, and another, and another, and swung his hand so hard into her nose the blood splattered over the rope binding Boy.

This made him weep even more.

Sad, pathetic, sack of shit.

"Knock it off, Cia," he said. "You're going to get hurt."

She charged at him again and he grabbed her by the throat, keeping her an arm's distance away.

"It's such a shame, such a waste, that someone with such potential, such venom, could not be a part of—"

She swung her hands onto his elbow, bending his arm and releasing her neck.

Right, enough of this talking.

It was distracting.

The Thoral's steps were creating a stronger shake of the ground. It was almost here, and everything had to be ready for it.

The trees surrounding the wall bustled.

It was about to arrive.

And she noticed it too. He saw her glance in its direction.

He saw the flicker of fear she tried to disguise seeping through the defiant sneer of her lip.

He saw her look at Boy as she realised it was futile.

That she had lost.

In another desperate lurch, she aimed a fist again, and he undercut her jaw.

She fell to the ground.

He mounted her back.

Tucked his arm around her neck and halted her ability to breathe.

He felt her suffocate and struggle.

The whole time, she locked her eyes with Boy's.

CHAPTER FIFTY

Boy was confused.

He was startled, he was perplexed, and he was terrified.

He was dumbfounded, irate and bombarded with disturbing thoughts.

And the most upsetting part of it was that he couldn't understand any of those emotions.

He just knew it distressed him, but all these other thoughts and feelings that came flooding through him—they only added to that distress by adding confusion that he couldn't understand was confusion.

Why was he here?

Why were they doing this?

Weren't they supposed to be nice people?

Graham had been nice. He'd taught Boy about people and what they say and what their body language is like and what that means and what you do when their faces have different expressions.

And now, none of it seemed to matter.

Because Rosy was about to die.

She was on her knees, Ryker behind her.

Mounting her.

Tucking his beefy arm around her dainty neck.

He placed the hand of that arm on the inside of his other arm's elbow, and he squeezed.

And Rosy could not breathe.

She batted at his arm; she grabbed at it, pulled it and pushed it and punched it but it was like a cat against a lion.

She wasn't breathing.

His Rosy wasn't breathing.

And he was about to lose her.

"No!" he shouted. "Leave her alone! Leave my Rosy alone!"

Why was Ryker doing this?

He just couldn't understand.

And he couldn't understand that he couldn't understand or why he couldn't understand and he didn't understand why that was.

He was just so scared.

His body shook, even though the rope entwined him so securely that his rigorous shaking was contained to a mild vibration.

The ground shook, and a roar grew closer and something was coming and was it coming for him?

Was that why they tied him up?

Because they wanted it to hurt him?

Why did they want it to hurt him?

Rosy's face was going blue, like a blueberry, and a little green as well. Her eyelids were drooping a little.

Was she going to die?

Why was she going to die?

Why was he doing this?

"Stop it! Stop it, now! Leave Rosy alone!"

They had taken him.

They had come into his home when Rosy wasn't looking and they had taken him and they had brought him here and those people, those who were so nice, who would help him, who would help Rosy—they put a hand around his mouth and dragged him away.

And he couldn't understand.

Then something happened that he understood, something that brought him right back to his lessons with Graham.

The end of the rope stuck out from behind his feet.

Rosy took it in one hand.

She looked up at him.

And she winked.

And she threw herself off the podium.

CHAPTER FIFTY-ONE

CIA DANGLED HELPLESSLY over the edge of the podium, clinging onto the rope.

Ryker hung off her, trying to keep his grip tight, trying to keep his arms around her neck.

One arm fell loose, and she could breathe again.

All of his weight pulled her down, dragged her away, and she gripped, gripped as hard as she could, moving her feet to the underside of the podium to help steady her.

Ryker's arm began to slip, wet from sweat, and he gripped tighter, grabbing a handful of skin and t-shirt.

His other hand reached up, going to grab her, going to use her to pull him up.

But she would not let him.

As soon as that arm came near, she reached out her open mouth and set her teeth around his fingers. He screamed, but he didn't let go, and it was just like biting a carrot, just like sinking her teeth in and chewing it off, and with similar force his hand went away but his forefinger remained in her mouth.

She spat it out, watching it disappear into the devastating drop.

She reached her open mouth to his other arm, blood flying away in the wind, and snapped her teeth around the one arm that still clung on.

With that, he let go, and in seconds he had gone, exiting her life as quickly as he had entered it. His scream disappeared into the shadows of the trees, and she was certain that she would never see him again.

But she was still clinging on to a rope that was becoming looser and looser.

And the upside-down view of a Thoral approaching was just as unsettling Ryker's desperate scream that had long since ended.

Using the rope to drag herself upwards, she pulled herself to the edge of the podium, threw an arm over, and hoisted herself up. She ignored the drop, slid onto her belly and dragged herself further on.

The Thoral was pounding the trembling earth; the trees shaking under the impact of its colossal feet.

The rope had loosened around Boy, but there was still plenty more bound around him. She forced herself to her feet, grabbed hold of it, and began untying him.

There was so much it felt like she was getting nowhere.

And Boy's cries were only getting worse. She didn't need to turn around to know the Thoral was now visible—she could see it in his eyes, hear it in the increased volume of his shrieks.

"Hey," she said. "Hey, Boy. Boy!"

He looked at her, his voice still mumbling as he cried.

"Keep saying it, yeah? The devil has departed, and you are not alone..."

He whispered the rest of the poem.

His eyes turned back over her shoulder and he kept

whispering it, getting quicker and quicker, the fear in his voice getting bigger and bigger.

She was almost there. Just another few loops to go.

The podium shook so hard she fell to her knees.

She looked behind herself, and there it was.

Horned, massive, bloody jaw and bloody fur.

Awaiting its sacrifice.

Cia did the penultimate loop, then the final one, and Boy was free.

Together, they turned and looked at it.

It approached.

Expectant.

Waiting.

"No," said Cia determinedly.

Its face curled, its large claw lifted and swiped forward toward the edge of the podium.

"There will be no sacrifice today."

She grabbed Boy's hand and sprinted to the stairs. She didn't slow down, didn't wait for his speed to match hers, didn't alter her determination—she sprinted and forced him to keep up.

Down the many steps they went, momentum carrying them quicker and quicker.

The Thoral's roar cast a large spray of wet wind over them and reverberated around the community.

They returned to the village hall and halted.

Cia turned to Boy and took his hand.

"Can we leave?" he asked, his voice so small, his cheeks wet, his face so delicate.

"Yes," Cia said. "Yes, we can. But not yet."

He went to moan, to do his thing when he covers his ears and closes his eyes and refuses to listen, but Cia was having none of it—not this time. Not here, not now.

She knew if they wasted a moment they would lose their lives along with the rest of the community.

This beast had not received its sacrifice.

And she knew it would not be long until everyone here paid the price.

"We need to hide," Cia said. "We need to hide, and we'll hide for a little while, maybe a few days, then we'll come out, and we'll leave."

He frantically shook his head.

"Please," she said. "Please, just trust me. Have I ever steered you wrong before?"

Maybe that was the wrong question—after all, she had allowed them to come here.

But Boy seemed to agree, and he shook his head.

She grabbed his hand and led him from room to room, searching, looking for the right place.

They passed a kitchen, and she led him in.

"Gather as much as you can," she told him, and went into the cupboards, grabbing packs of crisps and cans and bottles of water. In seconds, they both held piles of supplies.

The ground shook and a few cans dropped.

Then the ground shook again.

Harder, and quicker, the ground kept shaking and shaking.

The Thoral.

Then screeches of Masketes joined.

And, most terrifying of all, the elongated, disgusting, mortifying hiss of a Lisker.

"Come on," she urged, deciding this was enough food. They searched from room to room for a hiding place that would keep them safe, but she could see nothing sufficient.

If the mistake of trusting this community would be fatal, this was the moment she'd learn it.

But Boy was smart, and he impressed her by finding a room with a large built-in wardrobe.

"Well done!" she said.

She threw the supplies on the floor, then took the clothes from the wardrobe and threw them on the bed.

Screams decorated the silence outside of the room's window. Cia afforded herself a glance and regretted it, gagging at the sight of a woman being torn limb by limb by a group of baby Masketes.

She grabbed Boy, took him inside of the wardrobe and shut the door.

It was pitch black, and she wished she'd found matches.

Then she remembered it didn't matter if they were in a little darkness, so long as they were alive.

"Come here," she told Boy, and she pulled him close, wrapped her arms around him, and he wrapped his arms around her.

And that was where they stayed.

CHAPTER FIFTY-TWO

THE THORAL SNEERED down at the fleeing humans.

The offering that they had readied had been retracted.

The sacrifice, the meal—*gone.*

It lifted its head back in anger and let out an almighty roar—not just its average roar; an elongated roar, prolonging the shake of the community who quivered in response to the wrath.

The creatures responded.

A dozen Masketes screeched in the distance.

A Lisker's long, low hiss of sinister sibilance answered.

The Thoral swiped away the podium, collapsed the steps that fell in on themselves until they disappeared into dust and rubble.

It leapt over the nearby village hall and landed its claws on an insignificant patch of crops.

It roared again, and the people fled.

Oh, how the people fled.

Their protection fell—the only thing keeping them safe destroyed.

And they did not understand how to react. They were

not experienced with the outside world and nor were they trained for such an unprecedented emergency.

There were no people trying to hide, no people trying to fight.

They did not know you could do such a thing.

All they knew was panic.

Hysteria encapsulated the population, consuming every rapid movement. Mothers grabbed their children, fathers grabbed their families, and some cowards fled from their children and families to save themselves.

But this was just a single Thoral. A massive, ravenous beast, with blood dripping from its fangs, the length of its body greater than the height of their houses—but it was just one.

And then it wasn't.

The ground shook so hard no one could run, no one could keep their balance; they all collapsed as another Thoral leapt the walls, and another, and another, and another.

The bloodshed started.

All the Thoral had to do was swipe its open mouth down and catch multiple screaming humans.

It petrifies each and every one of them. It is one thing to hear a Thoral; it is one thing to be scared by the knowledge of it—but it is an experience you cannot replicate when you know that, despite your desperate fleeing, you stand no chance of survival.

What's more, you aren't just anticipating your death—you're anticipating your demise.

This isn't just a bullet in the head and down you go. This is looking down and seeing your body inside out.

This is being ripped apart while you endure the agony.

This is feeling the fangs in your body and the stream of their throat and the acid of their bellies.

And the Thorals were just the start.

Those that had taken shelter, that thought it would obscure them from the eyes of the Thoral, what with the Thoral being so high up, were not safe at all. The screeches of a dozen Masketes grew louder, and they pounded onto the ground, locked eyes with these poorly hidden families, and fed upon the parents as the children watched.

The children fled, but the baby Masketes were ready to practise their hunting. They gathered in a circle, taunted them at first, then ended their tears as they each took a limb and pulled and ripped and fed.

Then, as if the worst hadn't already happened, the few survivors who could do nothing but witness the remnants of their neighbours being discarded haplessly among the crops they had worked so hard on, they heard something.

A hiss.

And the rare sight of a serpentine creature appeared. The thickness of its body outdid the Thoral, the length of its body outdid multiple streets, and if its fangs didn't meet you, then the rough edges of its slithering body would slice through your back or your throat or anybody part straying from your body.

When the entire community had fallen, when it seemed as if the creatures had finished, when the few minutes it took to destroy years of growth had finished, they didn't leave.

They hunted.

There were still more, they could smell them.

They were locking the doors to their houses, as if that could do anything.

They were searching for loved ones.

They were even trying to mount the wall.

They were trying to hide.

But the community, unlike Cia, did not know how to

hide. They did not seek a wardrobe hidden in an obscure room; they simply closed a door and hid behind it.

This was not enough.

They knew nothing of these creatures or this world, and none of their fleeing would ever be enough.

And they all—every single last one of them—fell prey to the creatures.

And the creatures continued to devour every survivor until there was nothing left but streets of red and stiff, stunned faces.

NOW

CHAPTER FIFTY-THREE

IT HAS BEEN A LONG TIME, but the noises seem to have stopped.

The screams and the roars and the screeches and the hisses and the battering and the hollers of pain...they are long gone.

Cia has no idea how long they have been in there. They have been rationing food pretty well. The wardrobe stinks from the urine and excrement in the corner, but they have become used to it.

Cia has come to learn that you can truly get used to anything should the situation or environment call for it.

But now they are coming to the end of their food. Boy is getting restless, and Cia's hasn't seen daylight in so long.

She estimates it has been four, maybe five days. Give or take. There is no way of knowing, but she has attempted to keep track by counting out thirty minutes, getting a feel for what thirty minutes felt like, and estimating from there.

But it has been a long time, and she is sure they are safe.

Not that there is any way of knowing for certain—but her

instincts have helped her survive, and it is denying her instincts that allowed this community to condemn her and Boy to a fate that they escaped by luck.

It seems, despite the skills and rage that Cia used, that luck is the greatest asset needed to survive in this new world.

"I'm going to go make sure it's safe," Cia tells Boy. "You wait here."

She knows it's safe. The noises have long since stopped.

But she wants to see what remains for herself. She wants to adjust, to come to terms, to take it in before Boy has to endure the sights he would see on his way out.

She stands, the muscles in her legs so stiff, so unused. She opens the door and the smell of wooden furniture overwhelms her. Not that she's noticed it before, but it is in such contrast to what she's used to that it seems stronger.

"I'll be right back," she whispers, and closes the wardrobe door.

She creeps out of the room, and along the corridor, until she reaches the door of the village hall.

She pauses.

Places her hand on the door handle.

Listens.

She is bombarded with an onslaught of silence.

Drawn out, indestructible, unmistakable silence.

She steps outside and quickly covers her eyes. The sun hides behind clouds and it isn't particularly bright, but it still takes a while for her to adjust to any light at all.

Once she has, she steps into the streets, and witnesses what is left.

Blood has dried into the stone surface.

Some corpses she recognises, a few are even relatively intact, but most are just discarded pieces that the creatures didn't find tasty enough to devour.

"Hello?" she says, wondering if anyone will respond.

No one does.

I did it again.

She has condemned another community to death.

She has condemned them to being torn apart by the creatures.

She has condemned them to...

No.

She stops forcing herself to feel bad. She is telling herself this in hope she will feel guilty but, despite the sight, she doesn't.

Whether that is a good or bad thing, she doesn't know.

Whether the remnants of such violence should have more impact on her than a shrug of her shoulders is debatable.

She did what she did to survive.

For Boy to survive.

That is her purpose.

Not to fit a role in a community that no longer works, in a society that has long since been destroyed. She is not a warrior for others, nor is she a protector for the people.

She is a survivor.

And she has made sure Boy is a survivor.

And all this striving for another purpose, for something greater...

She had failed to realise.

I already have it.

So she looks over the few remaining faces and the discarded limbs and anything else that remains. She recognises little, but it doesn't matter; she is numb to every bit of it.

And she is not sad to leave this place behind.

All it has done is prove to her what she already knows.

That she is fine surviving day to day, out there.

Her and Boy together and alive is far, far greater reason to live than any community could ever give her.

AFTER

CHAPTER FIFTY-FOUR

Boy DEVOURED another bunch of blueberries, and it was as if nothing had ever happened.

Days of walking had resulted in a few incidents of having to hide from creatures, and a few incidents of having to run from loud noises, but their journey had been mostly peaceful.

And now, she tried to give Boy a bit of space. She sat on a log, yards away, knowing that she didn't need to be next to him all the time.

He wasn't a child anymore. He was a teenager. Different or not, he needed to grow, and she was helping him do that.

And then it happened again.

Sudden flashes.

Dalton appeared before him. She swiped for him, knowing he wasn't there, but she just pushed her hand through his belly and he didn't go.

This again?

She stood and turned away, but he was in front of her.

Looking at her.

Staring at her.

The man she'd killed.

She turned around and there was Hades.

He said nothing and shouted at the same time.

Why didn't you save me? he wanted to know.

Why did you kill me? asked Ryker.

Why did you kill your dad? asked her father.

She collapsed into a ball, buried her head, and whined until she couldn't hear anymore, until it drowned the voices out.

She tried saying the poem she had taught Boy but it did nothing. She just kept hearing them.

No matter how much she covered her ears, no matter how much she shouted over them, they just kept going.

Asking the same questions over and over again.

A panic attack, they said it was. And that was one thing she believed.

But that just sounded so simple. The label of panic attack, oh that's all, just snap out of it—it feels a lot tougher when everything you keep buried away pushes down on you, shouting and shouting and asking you the same questions.

"The devil has departed and you are not alone," she whispered to herself. "Take time to rebuild our love in our home."

But it wasn't enough.

Then there was one voice, a voice that broke through all of the shouting, delicate and shy but confident and determined, a voice she knew better than any other voice.

"Rosy," it said.

She tried not to cry.

"Rosy!"

A hand on her back.

She looked up.

They had all gone, every one of them.

All that remained was Boy, his smiling face beaming down at her, standing next to her, his hand on her back.

"It's okay, Rosy," he said.

And that was it.

That was all it took.

No therapy, no drugs, no facing what she had done.

Just Boy, telling her it was okay.

He held out his hand and helped her up, and they kept walking, together, hand in hand.

And that was all she needed.

BOOK FOUR: WHEN THE DEAD HAVE DECAYED IS OUT NOW

.

JOIN RICK'S READER'S GROUP AND GET TWO BOOKS FREE!

Join now at www.rickwoodwriter.com/sign-up

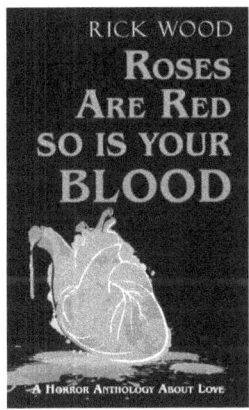

ALSO BY RICK WOOD

BOOK ONE IN THE SENSITIVES SERIES

THE SENSITIVES

RICK WOOD

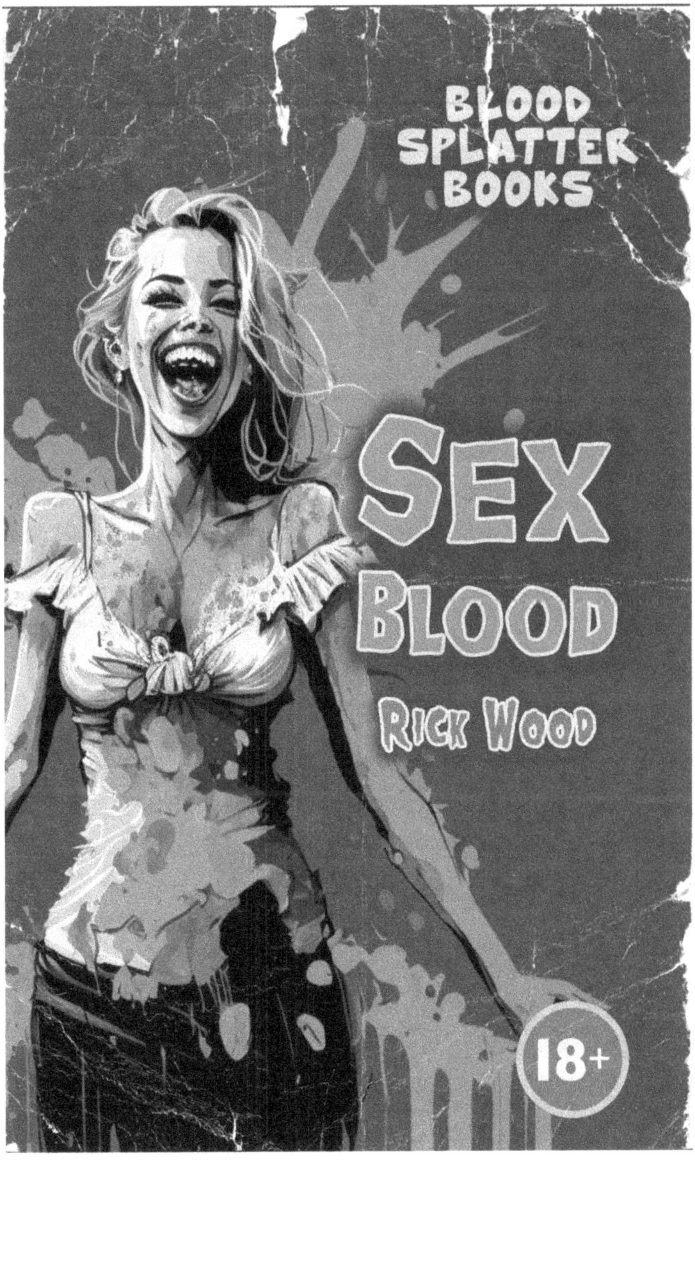
BLOOD
SPLATTER
BOOKS
SEX
BLOOD
RICK WOOD
18+

RICK WOOD

CHRONICLES
OF THE
INFECTED
BOOK ONE

ZOMBIE ATTACK

Milton Keynes UK
Ingram Content Group UK Ltd.
UKHW040136301123
433460UK00018B/297/J